Together Again

I longed to put my arms around Lenny, but I didn't. How could I when he had been the one to break up with me?

Our hands made contact, and he clasped mine in his. I looked at him and he smiled. "It's so nice here with you, Linda. I guess I forgot how much I liked being with you."

I felt a stab of pain, remembering how many other girls he had chosen to be with this summer instead of me. "What about Nancy and Toni and Chrissy. . . ?" I couldn't help asking, even though I knew it would ruin the mood.

He put his arm around me. "Forget them. None of them meant anything to me. I had to go out with other girls to find out if what we had was really special."

I wanted to let myself melt up against him, but part of me held back. "And what did you find out?"

He sighed. "That there's no one like you for me, Linda. No one. All those girls could be lumped together in one meaningless blob for all the difference they make. We're meant to be together, and that's all there is to it."

My defenses crumpled. "I want to be with you, too," I whispered, "but . . ."

"No buts," he said, bringing his face close to mine. And then he was kissing me, and I was kissing him back.

All For The Love Of That Boy

Linda Lewis

AN ARCHWAY PAPERBACK
Published by POCKET BOOKS
New York   London   Toronto   Sydney   Tokyo

AN ARCHWAY PAPERBACK *Original*

An Archway Paperback published by
POCKET BOOKS, a division of Simon & Schuster Inc.
1230 Avenue of the Americas, New York, NY 10020

ISBN: 0-671-68243-1

First Archway Paperback printing November 1989

10 9 8 7 6 5 4 3 2 1

AN ARCHWAY PAPERBACK and colophon are registered trademarks of Simon & Schuster Inc.

Printed in the U.S.A.

IL 7+

To Shelton,
who got everything started

All For The Love Of That Boy

Chapter
One

What do you say when you write a letter to the boy who used to be your boyfriend? To the boy you were going with off and on for almost an entire year and thought you were madly in love with? To the boy who dumped you before you went away to the country for the summer? In my mind, I still kept hearing the words he had said to me:

"I want you to believe, Linda, that no matter how difficult it is for the two of us, it's better we're away from each other for the summer. You can get to know some boys in the country, and I'll be able to do my thing here at home. When we meet again in September, we'll both have grown. Maybe we'll be ready to start a relationship again, or maybe we'll have drifted apart. But whatever happens, it'll be for the best. Do you agree?"

Did I agree? A stab of pain went through me just

1

thinking about it. Lenny Lipoff was the one I wanted, and I wanted him now. I knew perfectly well what the "thing" was that he wanted to do at home in New York City while I was away. He wanted to go out with other girls and find out what he had been missing during the time he had been going with me. The idea made me burn with jealousy.

But there was nothing I could do about the situation. I realized, painful as it was, that I was going to have to go through the summer without Lenny. I had no choice but to accept it. Accept it and wait and hope for the future.

"I agree," I somehow managed to say.

"Good," he said, grinning his mischievous grin that made my heart race. Lenny was more cute than handsome. He was tall and thin, with big brown eyes and brown hair that curled around an adorable, innocent-looking baby face. But Lenny was far from innocent. He was the prime wise guy, joker, and mischief maker in our neighborhood. If trouble was to be found, the chances were that Lenny had something to do with it. Lenny had a scar on the right side of his face that he liked to claim he received in a knife-fight. He was only kidding about that, but the truth remained that Lenny was entirely capable of getting someone mad enough to want to stab him.

Including me. Our relationship had been filled with stormy fights, breakups, and makeups. But Lenny had another side to him as well, a side he usually kept hidden. Lenny could be sweet and sensitive and feeling. He had more depth than I had found in any other boy. Sometimes Lenny could make me see things about myself that no one else could. When he talked, I could listen to his powerful, mesmerizing voice for hours.

I don't know what it was that attracted me to Lenny more—his wild and crazy side or his deep and sensitive one. I only know that I had fallen so deeply in love with him that he had become the center of my world. And then, right before the summer, he had broken up with me and started hanging around with a new group of boys and girls. He began throwing parties and seemed to be having the time of his life. It was as if I had never mattered to him.

Right before I left for the country, I had found out this wasn't the case. Lenny admitted to me that he really did care about me. But he also felt we were too young for the kind of relationship we had been having. I was just fifteen; he was turning seventeen. This was the time of our lives when we should be free, having fun, getting to know other people and ourselves. He didn't want to wind up too serious, getting married someday, and then regretting it. We were better off parting now and waiting to see how things would work out when we met again in September.

"Well, since we're parting as friends, will you write to me and let me know how you're doing?" Lenny had asked, once I voiced my agreement.

"Okay; that is, if you'll write back."

"Sure I will," he had promised. "But you write first. So, I'll see you in September. Have a great summer, Linda."

3

Then he had bent over and kissed me on my lips. It was just a light kiss, but it was still enough to set my heart hammering. Lenny always affected me that way. It was almost as if there were a strange force drawing me to him, a force too powerful for me to resist.

So now I found myself away in the country, a place where I didn't really want to be. My mother, who worked part-time in a school, was off for the summer, and my father wanted someplace to come to on weekends and for his vacation, so they had rented a summer cottage in the Catskill mountains, in a place called Eden Gardens. If you asked me, it sounded like a cemetery. My social life there was sure to be absolute death.

But nobody bothered to ask me. My parents claimed that the cottage would give our family a chance to "get out of the city and breathe some good, clean country air." It would give my brothers, Ira and Joey, who are eleven years old and twin pain-in-the-necks, a chance to go to day camp. It would give me a job as a CIT, or counselor-in-training, and a chance to "get good experience, make some money, and meet other nice young people."

Those were the excuses my parents gave me when they were trying to sell me on the idea of going away to the country for the summer. I knew perfectly well that the main reason they wanted me out of the city was to get me away from Lenny.

My parents had been against my relationship with Lenny from the start. They didn't like him because he had a fresh mouth and had trouble with his parents, who were separated, and with school. They never got to know Lenny well enough to find out his good points.

But I did. That's why I sat here now, on the porch of my cottage, struggling to come up with the perfect letter to Lenny. I didn't want to sound as if I cared too much or missed him like crazy, but I didn't want to come off as totally disinterested either. I decided to start with the humorous approach:

To my Dear, Sweet, Lovable, and *Cruel,* Exboyfriend Lenny,

You might be happy (then again you might not) to know I arrived at the country without our vehicle's crashing into such obstacles as trees, people, stray cats, railroad trains, or other vehicles. However, there is a chance that my sorrowful life will be snuffed out while trudging through the wilderness here en route to the post office to mail this letter. In case of such an occurrence, I hope you will mourn me for at least one day before throwing another party.

I read this beginning over and decided I liked it. It had a nice, devil-may-care ring to it, with just enough of a sense of the tragic to make Lenny feel a bit guilty for his treatment of me. And then there was the dig about his throwing a party, a reference to the one he had had the night before I left for the country, the one to which he didn't invite me.

Having said this, I decided to write something that sounded both sensible and mature.

Actually, I'm really glad we broke up when we did. Now we can meet new people and have fun without feeling guilty or sneaky. We can find out if we really like each other. In September, we can see how things stand with us. We can decide then if we want a relationship as boyfriend and girlfriend, as good friends, or as mere casual acquaintances, nodding hello when passing on the street, all traces of our past feelings gone forever. I hope that no matter what happens, we'll never become enemies.

After adding this flowering-sounding stuff, I concluded by telling him how beautiful and peaceful the country was, and how there seemed to be quite a few interesting teenagers staying in our group of cottages. I was looking forward to getting to know them and having a great summer.

This description of the country was stretching the truth a bit. Oh, the country was beautiful all right, and peaceful. From my spot on the porch I could see a stretch of the Catskills outlined against the sky and hear birds singing in the mighty oak trees that shaded the cottage. Off to one side was an apple orchard, its trees heavy with ripening fruit. Behind the cottage was a playground, where some of the younger children were swinging and sliding, and a field where my brothers were already tossing a ball back and forth to my father. From inside the cottage, which had two bedrooms and a kitchen that also had a bed, drifted the smells of the grilled cheese sandwiches my mother had made for lunch.

The problem was with the "interesting teen-agers" I had written about. Except for one boy, Pat, who lived in the cottage next door, I had met none of them. And Pat was only fourteen, a senior camper, too young to even be a CIT, much less of romantic interest to me.

Pat was interesting, however. He came from France and was spending the summer with his cous-ins, whose family had rented the cottage. He had been in America before and spoke good English.

As I was thinking of Pat, he made an appearance in front of my door. "Hi, Linda," he said in his cute, slightly accented voice. "What are you do-ing?"

"Finishing a letter." I licked the envelope and sealed it quickly. "I was planning to mail it at the post office. Do you know where it is?"

"In town, right next to the general store." He smiled impishly. "I'll walk you if you want."

I was going to tell him not to bother, but then thought better of it. Pat was young, but he was a boy and a pretty cute one at that. None of the other kids in the area had come around to try to make me feel welcome. I might as well talk to Pat. "Okay, why not?" I shrugged.

I told my father that I was leaving, and Pat and I walked down the road that separated our group of cottages from the main section on the other side. As we walked, Pat filled me in on what he knew about Eden Gardens.

"That's the recreation center up the hill to the

right,'' he pointed out. ''We'll be meeting there at nine o'clock Monday morning for the start of camp. The center has a snack bar, too, so most of the teenagers also hang out there at night.''

''Oh? Have you been hanging around with them?''

''No,'' Pat admitted. ''I only got here three days before you did, but no one even bothered to come say hello. I was told there are two boys who are CIT's, five CIT girls, including you, and four girls and two boys in the senior group with me. They've all been coming to Eden Gardens a long time and know each other. The new people who come usually wind up in the area known as the 'annex'—the cottages on our side of the road. From what I hear, the rest of the place regards us as outcasts.''

''Great,'' I said sarcastically. ''Not only do my parents drag me off to the country against my will, but I'm already considered socially inferior before anyone meets me.''

''Not by me,'' Pat surprised me by saying. ''I always admired older women!'' He flashed me a sensual look.

I didn't know how to take this. ''Oh, so at the ripe old age of fifteen, I'm already considered an older woman!''

He laughed. ''No, you don't understand; it's a compliment. In France, women are considered to grow even more beautiful as they mature. They have worldliness and become skilled in the ways of love, if you know what I mean.'' He winked at me.

He looked so cute I couldn't help laughing. ''I know what you mean. But I'm sorry to disappoint you. The only skill I've acquired in the ways of love is the experience I had this year with my boyfriend, Lenny. And I couldn't have been too successful in that department, because he broke up with me before I left for the country. He wants to be free to date other girls.''

"Well, he should be able to do that. But that's no reason to give you up. In France, we have our own special girlfriend, but see others as well. Why limit yourself to just one flower when you can gather a whole bouquet? And you, you can do it as well as he can.''

"I know." I sighed. "But I really don't want to. I guess it would be better if I could take relationships lightly, but I can't. As long as I'm in love with Lenny, I don't even have any desire for anyone else.''

"No? That's too bad.'' Pat shook his head in a gesture of sadness. "But still, I don't give up. Keep—how you say it—an open mind, Linda. You never can tell what this summer has in store for you!''

Chapter

Two

Despite Pat's words of encouragement, Eden Gardens was pretty much the way I feared it would be. I didn't meet the other counselors until camp started. When I did, they were far from friendly.

I guess the girls weren't happy about having another female around to compete for the attention of the two CIT boys, Roger and Evan, because all I got from them was an icy "Hello." As for the boys, once they found I wasn't about to play up to them and mush all over them the way the other girls did, they didn't pay me much attention, either.

The group I was assigned to was called the Tumbleweeds. There were over twenty little kids, ages five to seven, under the direction of Tess, the senior counselor. Tess was a teacher during the school year, so she knew what she was doing. By watching and listening to her, I found I could learn a lot about dealing with kids.

Roger was also a CIT for the Tumbleweeds, and it didn't take long to discover that he was a complete lamebrain. He messed up even simple stuff like art projects that merely required helping kids glue seashells onto cigar boxes. Somehow, all those kids helped by Roger wound up with their boxes glued completely shut. Roger couldn't keep scores right when the kids played kickball; he spilled the juice at snacktime; and he ate so many cookies, there weren't enough left for the kids.

Once Tess discovered what a jerk Roger was, she began giving him less and less to do, and she gave me more and more. I wound up having to do most of Roger's job as well as my own.

I didn't really mind that so much. I never liked to sit around doing nothing; I preferred to keep busy. It made the days go by faster and brought me closer to the time I could be with Lenny again.

Not that I had any guarantee that Lenny and I would wind up back together. He had made no promises to me before I left. I knew he would be going out with other girls while I was away, and it was always possible he would fall for one of them. Each day, I waited anxiously for a letter from the city so I could find out what was going on. I had written to my closest friends, Fran Zaro, Roz Buttons, and Donna Fiori, the day after I had written to Lenny. I was bound to hear from one of them soon.

Each day, when camp let out at five o'clock, I rushed to the rec hall, where the mailboxes were located. Each day I found nothing. I struggled not to show my disappointment. To be stuck in the country and cut off from everything going on in the city was pure torture for me. Why was the mail so darn slow?

Finally, on Friday, there were two letters sitting in my box. The one on top was from Fran—I could tell her messy handwriting anywhere. Slowly, I slid it off the bottom letter so I could see the return address. Was it? It was from Lenny! Joyfully, I rushed from the rec hall, looking for a secluded place to read my mail without being disturbed.

I found it in the apple orchard near my cottage. There was a big old tree with thick branches that hung low enough for me to grab. I hoisted myself up and settled in a comfortable nook created by two large branches that came together against the trunk. Anxiously, I ripped open the letter from Lenny first.

His letter wasn't very long, and it wasn't very satisfying. He started out by parroting the opening I had written to him:

To my Dear, Sweet, and Lovable, but not too *Cruel* Ex-girlfriend Linda.

He told me he was glad I had arrived at the country safe and sound, and he hoped I would like it there. Then he began to tell me what a great time he was having in the city.

It seemed that summer vacation was drawing kids from other neighborhoods to our crowd's hangout— a wall that overlooked the baseball field of the park.

There was always someone new showing up, always something interesting happening. Of course, summer school and his part-time job at a drugstore were far from exciting, but he and his friends more than made up for it at night when they hung around the wall or the poolroom, or organized a card game. Sometimes they had so much fun they would stay out all night. Not only that, he had dates with three different girls coming up. He hoped I was having as much fun this summer as he was.

When I finished reading, I sat there staring at the letter. My first reaction was one of anger. The nerve of Lenny to write me a letter like that! The nerve of him to tell me what a great time he was having in the city without me! The nerve of him to rub it in that he was going out with three girls in one week! How could he?

I took some deep breaths and finally began to calm down. After all, I had asked Lenny to tell me all about what he was doing in the city, and he had done exactly that. I would rather know the truth, painful as it was. Then at least I could make up my mind how to deal with it.

And, when I thought about it, Lenny was reacting just the way I would expect him to act. During the year we had been going together, one of the biggest problems we had to deal with was that Lenny felt torn between me and his friends. Some of Lenny's friends didn't have girlfriends. Those that did weren't as involved as we were, and they always teased Lenny about spending too much time with me. So I guess it was natural for him to be running around with his friends as much as possible now that he was free.

It was probably natural for him to want to go out with a lot of different girls, too. Lenny had told me that the worst thing about going steady was that we would wind up wondering what we had missed by not finding out what other people were like to date. So here he was, making sure he found out.

Actually, this wasn't so different from the way Lenny had acted the other times he had broken up with me. He would always start by going out of his way to prove he could have a good time. He would act wild and crazy and happy and carefree, as if he were glad to be rid of the burden that was me.

And then he would burn out. As soon as I would start making a life for myself, he would realize that it was me he wanted after all, then tell me he was sorry for the hurt he had caused me, and ask me to be his girlfriend again. And each time I would take him back, so happy to have him that I would forgive him anything.

But three girls in one week! As I thought about it I felt hot anger beginning to take control of me again, but I shook it off. I couldn't do anything about the situation, and besides, I still had Fran's letter to read. Maybe she had some information that Lenny hadn't given me.

I opened Fran's letter and couldn't believe what I saw. She had typed the whole thing on a long sheet of pink two-ply toilet paper!

I had to laugh. That Fran was such a nut! Short, with wild frizzy black hair and a sprinkling of freckles, Fran could be actually pretty when she took off

the thick glasses that hid her long-lashed violet
eyes. Fran had been going with her boyfriend,
Danny Kopler, who had at one time lived in my
apartment building, for about one and a half years
Recently, they had had problems in their relationship, too, mostly because Fran wanted to go out
with other boys, and Danny was not happy about
this. The fact that Danny's parents had moved away
from our neighborhood in Washington Heights and
out to Queens had put more stress on their relationship. And now Danny, who was a mathematical
genius, would be going away to college in Massachusetts. Fran was torn between letting go of him
so she could have her freedom and holding on to
him because she thought she still cared.

Fran's letter reflected her mixed-up state of mind:

Dear Linda,

If you think you're lonely up in the country,
you should see what it's like in the city for me!
I'm surrounded by people who don't understand me. My parents are hopeless, but what's
worse is what's happening with Dan. He
doesn't want me to date anyone else, ever, but
just sit in the house all day with him. On top of
that, he makes nasty remarks about every boy
who shows me the slightest attention. When I
tell him it's ridiculous not to date anyone else,
he throws a fit. It's awful! He seems to like me
more than I want or deserve to be liked.

I don't want to see Dan unhappy, but I do
want to live my own life and not be tied down
years before I'm ready to find a person to

marry. I feel like I'm going insane. What do
you think I should do about Dan?

What did I think she should do about Dan? What
a question! I would love to be in Fran's situation
right now. I would like nothing better than to have
Lenny want me so much that he didn't want me to
go out with other boys. There was no one I wanted
to date, anyhow. If I were Fran, I would just love
Danny back and be happy doing it!

Fran went on to tell me about some of the boys
she had managed to flirt with when Danny wasn't
around. Then she finally got to the subject of
Lenny:

I saw Lenny the other day when his friend,
Joel Fudd, invited me to join a bunch of kids
that were going up to his house. Lenny acted
like a real hotshot, dancing with one girl after
another, especially Nancy, who is very cute.
When he danced with me, he mentioned he was
taking Nancy out this weekend, and also Toni,
and Chrissy. I'll try to get to know the girls
better and find out what they think of him, but
what's really important is: What do you think
of him now? Do you still like him? Don't waste
your time; he's only interested in having fun
and doesn't care whom he hurts. Forget the
memories and see him as he really is.

Fran's words really hit home. The picture of
Lenny, dancing and flirting with these new girls,
taking them out on dates, and making out with them

was more than I could bear. And all this while I was rotting here in the country with nothing to do after camp but read and eat and hang around with kids who were all younger than I was. What a disgusting situation!

I wrote back to Fran that I wasn't sure how I felt about Lenny at this point, and that she should listen to her heart in deciding what to do about Danny. I wrote Lenny a long, philosophizing letter about how it was great to be having fun, but he should think about where it was all going to lead him.

And I made up my mind that I would have to stop avoiding the other CITs after camp and start developing some sort of social life. I knew the CITs, along with some of the senior boys and girls, were planning a trip this week into the town of Monticello to see a movie. I had said I wasn't interested in going, but now I would have to find some excuse and tell them I had changed my mind.

Lenny was obviously spending little time thinking of me back in the city. There was no way I was going to continue wasting my summer pining away over him.

I could see right away that this trip to the movies was not the solution to my social problems. It was the perfect illustration of the fact that it's possible to be lonelier in the middle of a crowd of people than it is by yourself.

Pat was supposed to have come with us, but at the last minute he had to babysit for his little cousins and couldn't go. So there was nobody in the group of seven girls and three boys I felt comfortable with.

I was the last girl to board the bus. All the others were paired off two to a seat, so I sat down by myself. Since there were three boys and the seats only held two people, Roger sat down next to me.

This earned me jealous stares from the other girls and remarks such as, "Don't you have enough of Roger all day long, Linda? Do you have to hog him at night, too?"

I was about to mention that I had more than enough of Roger during the day, and anyone who wanted to sit next to his creepy, lamebrained body was more than welcome to it, but I thought better of it. This way, I could write to Lenny that I went to the movies with Roger and only be stretching the truth a little.

"Very funny," was all I said. Roger blushed and immediately turned to talk to the boys in the row behind us about such exciting matters as the latest batting statistics of the New York Yankees. The other girls began whispering among themselves and giggling. I was sure they were talking about Roger and the other boys, so I had no interest in their conversation, either. I might as well have been by myself for all I had in common with this group of kids.

When we got to the movies I made sure to sit as far away from Roger as possible so as not to stir up any further animosity. After the movie was over, we had some time before our bus was due so we stopped in a store that had video games.

I never saw anything like it. The boys each went

to play a game and the girls all gathered around to watch them and make flirtatious remarks. None of the girls seemed to have the slightest interest in doing anything themselves; they were interested only in those three nerdy boys.

It was disgusting to see. Although I didn't really like video games, I decided it was preferable to play one than to stand around watching the girls watch the boys.

"I'm going down there to play a game," I said to no one in particular, pointing to an empty machine in a corner of the room. No one even acknowledged me, so I went over, put in my money, and began to play.

Actually, it was kind of fun. The game consisted of a mock road that you had to steer your car down as quickly as possible, avoiding all the obstacles that appeared along the way. I wasn't very good at first, but I found myself getting better. I became so engrossed in what I was doing that I didn't notice the other kids leaving the video area. When I had finished my game, I looked around to find that everyone else had disappeared!

"Hey, where is everyone?" I called. The only response was a few stares from strangers; no one I knew was there.

I looked at my watch. It was 10:55. The bus was due at 11:00 to take us back to Eden Gardens. I had my ticket, but I had no idea where the bus terminal was. I had spent my last quarter on the video game. If I missed the bus I couldn't even call anyone to come and get me. I'd be stranded here in Monticello, a perfectly strange town!

I felt panic overtaking me and raced outside the video store to see if I could spot the bus terminal. The street was deserted except for a few tough-looking characters hanging around the corner. There was nothing that looked like a bus terminal. A sick feeling of dread came over me. Anxiously, I returned to the video store. I would ask the clerk at the change booth. Anyone who worked in this town would have to know where the terminal was.

The clerk looked at me as if I were crazy when I asked for directions, then began to laugh. "The bus terminal? Where do you think you are anyway, kid? This is no big city with a fancy station. This *is* the bus terminal in this town. I sell tickets as well as supervise the video games. Go out the back door and you'll see where the buses stop!"

I looked at my watch and saw it was 10:59. I raced to the back door and got there just as the kids from Eden Gardens opened it. They had finally noticed I was gone and had come to look for me.

They bombarded me with angry remarks as soon as they saw me. "Where were you, Linda? Don't you say anything when you go off somewhere? What a dumb thing to do! We could have missed the bus looking for you!"

I tried to explain what had happened, but no one seemed interested in my explanations. Obviously, this night had done nothing to bring me closer to the other kids. I was going to have to find some other way to salvage the summer and prove I could have as good a time as Lenny could!

Chapter
Three

I made a few more efforts to become part of the group of teenagers at Eden Gardens, but nothing seemed to click for me. Roger and Evan were both such creeps they weren't even worth flirting with. And I had little patience for the girl counselors who swooned over them as if they were the last males on earth.

I was much more comfortable staying on my side of the road with Pat, his cousins, and my brothers. We would fool around together, and Pat would play French music on his tape recorder and teach me to dance the way they did in France.

I wrote to Lenny about this because it was the only thing I had worth writing about. In response, Lenny wrote me a letter saying that since I had started robbing cradles, he'd be happy to fix me up with his thirteen-year-old cousin when I got back to the city. I wrote back that Pat and I were just good friends, and not everyone could be as lucky as Lenny and have three dates with three different people in one week.

Lenny wrote back that none of the dates had amounted to anything. The girls were okay, but he wasn't interested enough to take them out again. He was getting bored with the summer and with doing the same old things with the same old people. He was looking forward to having me come home to liven things up again.

I couldn't believe what I was reading. When he first broke up with me, Lenny kept telling me how great the other girls were—how much more mature they were than I was, how they knew how to act like "ladies" and I didn't.

It was absolutely devastating to me to hear this. I had tried my best to be the kind of girlfriend Lenny wanted me to be. I really cared about him and wanted only good things for him. Of course I wasn't perfect, and sometimes I made mistakes and said or did dumb things that got him angry. But I certainly wasn't as bad as he had made me out to be, and the other girls couldn't possibly be so wonderful and perfect. Now it looked as if Lenny were starting to come back to reality. It looked as if he were starting to remember the good things we had together and starting to miss them. I didn't want to get my hopes up too high, but I was getting the feeling that he might want me back again.

The letters I got from my friends seemed to confirm what I was feeling. Then my hopes really began to rise the night he called me on the phone.

I was sitting out in the apple orchard reading a great book, when I heard my brothers calling my name: "Linda! Linda, where are you?"

At first I was tempted to remain in my tree, where they couldn't see me. Usually, if my brothers were looking for me it meant either they wanted to pester me or that my mother needed me to do some mundane chore. I wasn't in the mood for either one. Yet, this time, something told me to reveal myself.

I swung down from my tree. "Here I am. What do you want?"

"We don't want anything," said Ira.

"But you might want to pick up the telephone," finished Joey. My brothers often did that—one would start a sentence and the other would finish it. It was probably because they were twins and together so much. "There's a call for you."

"A call for me? But who?"

"We don't know," said Ira.

"But it's long distance, so you'd better hurry," added Joey.

Long distance! My heart began to beat wildly. It had to be Lenny; it just had to be! I had sent him the number of the pay phone our cottages shared in case he needed to get in touch with me.

I practically flew to the phone. "Hello!" I said breathlessly.

"Hello!" His voice boomed across the line. "What are you doing up there? Robbing French cradles?"

I heard his laugh and it sent shivers through me. "No-oo. I was just off reading a book," I said,

23

failing to take the opportunity to try to make him jealous by building up Pat.

"So then you're behaving yourself?"

"Of course I'm behaving myself. Which is more than I can say for what I've been hearing about you."

"Oh? And what is it you've been hearing?"

"Why don't you tell me what you've been doing, and then I'll let you know if it's the same stuff I've heard about," I countered.

He laughed again. "Some things are better off not discussed on the phone. Why don't we wait until I see you in person?"

"That's an awfully long time to wait—more than another month," I pointed out.

"Maybe not. I was thinking I could use a break from the city. Would you want me to take a bus up for a day to visit you?"

Would I want him to? I had to restrain myself from shouting with joy. "Well, I guess that would be nice." I struggled to keep my voice calm. "Come on the weekend when I don't have to work at camp. But it's a long trip for one day. Why don't I ask my mother if you can stay over. There's an extra bed in the kitchen for company, and I'm sure she won't mind if you spend the night."

"Are you kidding? Your parents can't stand me," he protested. But he agreed to let me ask them anyway. We arranged for him to call me again the next week to find out if it would be okay for him to come the following weekend. Then he was out of money and had to get off the phone.

I stood staring at that telephone long after he had

hung up. Lenny had called me and wanted to see me. I could hardly believe it was true. Even though I didn't want to let my hopes get too high, it had to mean he was interested in me again. Now, if only I could get my parents to let him come!

My parents were basically okay. They had good values and all that stuff, but they had one major fault. When it came to anything to do with boys and sex, their ideas were from another century. To them, the only thing that was important was for me to get a good education, and they were convinced that my interest in boys would interfere with this. The fact that I had managed to keep my grades high despite my social life did nothing to change their minds.

They probably wouldn't have been happy about my having a serious relationship with anyone at my age, but the fact that it was Lenny made it much worse. Lenny's big mouth had earned him a reputation for being wild and crazy, and my parents didn't like the kinds of things they heard about him. They didn't like to see me hurt all those times he broke up with me. And most of all they didn't like the fact that even though Lenny was smart, he wasn't doing well in school. After all, what kind of future could he have without a good education?

My parents didn't like Lenny, but they also were aware of how unhappy I had been with my social life here in the country. I knew it bothered them that I was so lonely here.

I took advantage of this when I asked them to let him come visit. I assured them he wasn't coming up as my boyfriend but as a friend to cheer me up because I was so lonely. Then I held my breath, waiting for their reply.

My mother sighed, shook her head of short black hair, and said, "It's up to your father."

My father frowned, pulling his bushy eyebrows together over blue-green eyes that were much like mine. I could tell that he wasn't too happy with my mother for transferring the decision to him. "Well, dear, it's really up to you. Having a guest is no trouble to me, but it is extra work for you."

"It's not the extra work that's the problem," my mother began.

"Good, then that settles it," I interrupted. I could see that this conversation might go back and forth forever, with neither one wanting to be the first to say yes or no. "Since Lenny won't be extra work, there should be no problem at all. Is a week from Saturday okay with you?"

My parents looked at each other, but neither could come up with a good reason why Lenny shouldn't be allowed to come. "As good as any," my mother said reluctantly.

"Great! I'll tell Lenny when he calls me, and I'll send him a bus schedule. And thanks, Ma, Daddy. Now I finally have something to look forward to this summer!"

As much as I looked forward to Lenny's visit, I was also apprehensive about it. What would it be like to see him after all this time apart? What if I found I didn't like him anymore? Even worse, what if he found he didn't like me? What would we say to one another now that we were no longer going together but just friends?

The days dragged by, but the Saturday of his visit finally arrived. The first few rays of light found me already awake, watching the minutes flash on the digital clock. Each minute brought me closer to the time of his arrival.

Finally, I got out of bed and got dressed. I chose a blue, turquoise, and white print shirt I knew Lenny liked. It brought out the blue of my eyes, which were big and definitely my best feature. They made up for my nose, which was one size too large for my face. And my summer tan made my skin, which tortured me by breaking out at all the wrong times, look much better. I brushed my shoulder-length light brown hair until it shone. As a whole the picture wasn't too bad, I thought as I gazed into the mirror. I only hoped Lenny would like what he saw.

The bus must have been early because Lenny was already sitting on the steps of the general store near the bus stop when I arrived. As soon as I saw him I felt a rush of warmth go through my body, and my heart began to pound. Why was it that Lenny always affected me this way? I didn't want him to have this power over me, for with it came the power to hurt.

"Hi!" He grinned when he saw me. He looked so cute I could hardly stand it. He was wearing a new blue shirt and jeans, and white sneakers. His smooth skin was bronzed from the sun, and his warm brown eyes positively glowed. I wanted to run to him and throw my arms around him and hold him and kiss him.

But I couldn't. Lenny had broken up with me.

He had decided he no longer wanted to be my boyfriend. I couldn't let him know how badly I ached to feel his arms around me once again.

"Hi." I struggled for some bright and witty thing to say. All I could do was come up with the obvious. "How was your trip?"

"Okay. Of course it was pure torture to get up so early, but the ride through the country was really pretty." He looked me over carefully, and I could feel myself blushing. "You look good. I think you put on a little weight."

I could have died. The last thing I wanted Lenny to notice was that I'd gained weight. It was all that hanging around the cottage at night with nothing to do but eat that had done it. I made a mental note to diet for the rest of the summer.

"It looks good on you," he added quickly. "It's in just the right places. You're getting some curves to your figure."

"Oh." That made me feel better. "Well, you look good, too."

We stood there a moment, smiling awkwardly at each other. "Well, aren't you going to show me around?" he asked. "There must be more to this fascinating country hideaway, complete with French lovers, than this."

I couldn't help laughing, and that broke the ice between us. For the entire walk back to Eden Gardens, we had plenty to say to each other. I told him all about the country and pointed out the few things of interest along the way. He told me about the city and talked about the kids that hung out on the park wall now and some of the things they had done. But he carefully avoided mentioning anything to do with his relationships with girls. I managed to control myself and keep from questioning him about this. It wasn't the right time. Yet.

The next big hurdle was having Lenny face my family. Lenny felt very uncomfortable around them because he knew none of them approved of him. We stayed away from my cottage as long as possible, playing racquetball on the courts, sitting by the pool, swinging on the swings. But as it grew close to lunchtime I knew we could no longer postpone the inevitable. My mother had told me she was making the main meal for lunch and I'd better be home with Lenny by 12:30 sharp.

They were all in the kitchen when we got there. My father was reading the paper. My mother was checking the chicken baking in the oven. My brothers—miracle of miracles—were actually helping to set the table.

When Lenny and I came to the door they all stopped what they were doing and stared at us. We stared back. It was as if everyone were frozen in a state of suspended animation.

Lenny was the first to break the spell. "Ahem!" He cleared his throat nervously. "Good afternoon, Mr. and Mrs. Berman. I want to thank you for inviting me here to the country. It was very nice of you."

"You're welcome." My mother managed to squeeze out a tight smile. "Why don't you go to the bathroom and wash up now? I'm sure you must be dirty and dusty from your trip."

I was so embarrassed. What a thing for my

mother to infer, that Lenny was dirty. I couldn't believe she had said that!

Fortunately, Lenny seemed to take it in stride. "Sure, Mrs. Berman," he said politely. "If you'll just show me where it is."

My mother directed him. Then she came back and whispered to me. "What took you so long to get here, Linda? I thought at least you'd have the consideration to come home early and help with lunch. Look, your brothers even had to set the table."

My brothers even had to set the table. Big deal! They were perfectly capable of helping out more often if my mother wouldn't treat them as precious, fragile infants. But I knew this was no time for me to voice my opinion. "I'll make the salad, Ma," I volunteered.

"Fine." You can wash your hands off in the kitchen sink since that boy is in the bathroom."

I bit down on my lip. I hated it when my parents called Lenny "that boy." They knew perfectly well what his name was. Why did they have to dislike him so much?

Conversation at the table could only be described as strained. My father, who is quiet under the best of circumstances, said nothing. My brothers, the little creeps, made periodic wisecracks about how it was too bad there weren't more boys up here or that there was so much competition among the girls—stuff I would never have let slip by. But now I was forced to laugh and pretend my brothers were just being cute.

Fortunately, my mother was never at a loss for

words. Her main conversation centered around the food. "Take another piece of chicken, Lenny. How do you like the potatoes cooked this way? It's one of my favorite recipes. Maybe you'd like to finish the peas; they're as sweet as sugar!" Have some more, have some more, have some more.

Usually my mother drove me crazy when she started pushing food, but today I was grateful for it. Just when we seemed destined to sink into silence, Mom was there to offer something else.

After Lenny had eaten all Mom could stuff into him, he got up to take his plate to the sink. This really impressed my mother. "See, Ira and Joey," she said to my brothers. "There's nothing wrong with boys helping out in the kitchen."

"Oh, you mean Lenny is a boy?" Joey wisecracked.

"It's too bad there aren't more boys up here so Linda could have a basis of comparison," added Ira needlessly.

"It doesn't matter. No real boy would be interested in Linda anyway," concluded Joey.

That was it for me. I had sat quietly all through the meal listening to my brothers' remarks and holding back my temper. But these last comments pushed me beyond the limits of my self-control.

"That's enough from you creeps!" I stood up from the table and grabbed Joey, who was closest to me, by the collar. "One more wise-guy remark and I'll wring your little neck!"

Joey immediately grabbed at his neck and began to choke and sputter, playing this scene for all the sympathy he could get. "My throat! My throat!

31

She's choking me! She's viscious! She's trying to kill me!''

"Linda! Let go of your brother this instant!" My mother fell for his act and came rushing to Joey's defense. She bent over and examined the brat's neck as if there was something really wrong with it. "I can't imagine what's gotten into you, attacking your brother this way. And in front of a guest, too! Or perhaps having your friend around is bringing out the worst in you!"

That did it. Poor Lenny had done nothing but be nice and polite, and he still wound up being blamed for everything.

"How could you say that, Ma? Didn't you hear what Joey and Ira said to me? They're the ones who bring out the worst in me! And this choking business is all a big act. I didn't even hurt Joey, as you can see by the fact that his big mouth works just fine!"

"Enough of this!" My father, who had been unhappily observing this interchange, broke in. Dad is basically quiet, but when he loses his temper, forget it! And he looked as if he were on the verge of losing his temper now.

Mom must have noticed that, too, because she made an unexpected move to make peace. "Linda, why don't you take your guest outside so he can enjoy the country air while he has the opportunity. I'll take care of the dishes today."

"You will? Great! Let's go, Lenny." I grabbed him by the elbow and steered him outside before my mother could change her mind. Washing the dishes was a chore I almost always got stuck with.

My mother must have wanted to get rid of us pretty badly to let me get away without doing them!

It was only when we were outside, safely out of sight and sound of my family, that I looked to Lenny for his reaction. "Sorry about that scene at the table," I apologized.

Fortunately, he chose to take this good-naturedly. "Scene? That was nothing," he laughed. "You haven't been at my house when my mother gets upset about something. But there's one thing that dinner with your family has convinced me to be grateful for."

"What's that?"

"Being an only child. Your brothers are too much for even me to handle!"

"Aren't they awful?" I agreed. "I can't wait until they start liking girls so I can give it back to them. But, actually, my brothers wound up doing us a favor. They got us out of the cottage fast, and got me out of doing the dishes, too!"

"Well, now that we've escaped, what would you like to do this afternoon?" Lenny asked.

"Well, we could go swimming, or take a walk in the woods somewhere, or—"

"A walk sounds good, if you know a place we could be alone."

"I know a perfect place! There's this little path through the woods. No one ever goes there, and it's beautiful!"

We walked down the road to where the path began. It started out very narrow, and the going was rough over rocks and through overhanging branches, so we had to make our way one at a time.

Walking that way, it was too difficult to carry on a conversation, so we went along in silence. After a while, the vegetation changed from deciduous to pine forest, the path broadened, and we were able to walk side by side.

Still we kept silent. The day was too perfect, the forest too beautiful to mar with words. The sky was a vivid blue, broken only by a scattering of cottony clouds. The sun shined through the towering pines, casting softly-changing shadows. The only sound was the rustling of the branches in the summer breeze and the occasional calling of a passing bird. The air shimmered with an almost magical intensity and was heavy with the sweet scent of pine.

We walked together, arms brushing, shoulders occasionally touching. I was very aware of Lenny's nearness. I longed to put my arms around him, but I didn't. How could I when he had been the one to break up with me and say he no longer wanted me? How could I when I didn't really know if he wanted me now?

We walked until we reached a clearing on a hill where there was a rock formation cushioned by a layer of moss and pine needles that created a natural chair. "Let's sit here." I whispered so as not to break the spell.

As we sat, our hands made contact, and he clasped mine in his. I looked at him and he smiled. "It's so nice being here with you, Linda. I guess I forgot how much I liked being with you."

I felt a stab of pain, remembering how many other girls he had chosen to be with this summer instead of me. "What about Nancy and Toni and Chrissy, and all the others whose names I don't even know?" I couldn't help saying, although I knew it would ruin the mood.

But Lenny wasn't about to let it be ruined so easily. "Forget them. None of them meant anything to me. I had to go out with them to find out if it could be the same with other girls as it was with you or if what we had was really special." He put his arm around me when he said that.

I sucked in my breath. It felt so good to have his arm around me again. I wanted to let myself melt up against him, but part of me still held back. "And what did you find out?"

He sighed. "That there's no one like you for me, Linda. No one. All those girls could be lumped together in one meaningless blob for all the difference they make. It's only when I'm with you that I totally come alive. We're meant to be together, and there's no use fighting it. I've tried often enough now to know. I learned my lesson. I want to go with you, and that's all there is to it!"

When I heard these words, any defenses I had built up crumpled. Any thoughts of telling him that it would be nice to continue dating him, but we really shouldn't start going together again because we would only run into more problems were blown away with the summer breeze.

I was defenseless against Lenny, and I knew it. I wanted him so badly that nothing else mattered. I could talk about being cautious and playing it cool fine when he wasn't around. But once he touched me and held me in his arms, I was totally overwhelmed by my all-consuming love for him.

"I want to go with you, too," I whispered. "But—"

"There are no buts," he said, bringing his face close to mine. And then he was kissing me, and I was caught up by the wonderful taste of him, and I was kissing him back. And all the pain of our breakup, all the loneliness, and all the longing were wiped out by that one sweet kiss.

We stayed there, among the pines, for a long time that afternoon, making out with more intensity and passion than we ever had before. And we talked as well, about the strengths and weaknesses of our relationship and the mistakes we had made in the past, such as getting too involved with one another, trying to change each other, and telling the other person what to do. We decided that in the future our goal would be to find a balance, a state where we could love and care for and enjoy each other, but also let go and allow each other to be individuals in our own right. We decided it would be best if we didn't "go steady," but kept the freedom to date other people if we pleased.

I knew a lot of the things we said were similar to things we had told each other in the past when we got back together after breakups, and we hadn't been able to stick to them before. But we had never gone through such a long, hard separation before. This time, we would learn from our experiences.

This time, when I got back to the city, we would do things right.

Chapter

Four

It's strange, but once the rest of the kids in the country found out that I really did have a boyfriend, they began to look at me differently. When I had needed them at the beginning of the summer to make me feel I belonged and to get my mind off how much it hurt to have been rejected by Lenny, they had wanted no part of me. Now that the summer was drawing to a close and my mind was focused on going back to the city, they started taking an interest in me.

I was invited to come to the snack bar at night and included in plans to go out with them for dinner at a Chinese restaurant to celebrate the end of camp. It was as if providing proof that I really did have a boyfriend gave me a status I hadn't had before. Suddenly, I was good enough to be part of the "in group" of kids who lived on the right side of the road at Eden Gardens.

At first I was so grateful to be accepted that I crossed the road to hang out with them at night. But I soon discovered I had been missing nothing by staying over on my side. As a group, the girls were still pretty boring; their main interests revolved around Roger and Evan, neither of whom would be worthy of such attentions if they hadn't been the only boys around. I went along with them to the restaurant and attended the good-bye party in the rec hall, just to be sociable. But I realized I still preferred the company of Pat and the kids on my side of the road, even though two of them were my own brothers.

None of this was really important to me now, anyhow. I was counting the days until I got back to New York to be with Lenny, my real friends, and our crowd.

I told this to my father on that glorious day when we started packing things to take back to the city. His reply to me really shook me up.

"Be very careful about putting so much emphasis on this 'crowd' you think is so important, Linda. It won't be long before all those kids are going off in their own separate directions, and they won't even mean anything to you."

I stared at him. My father was a serious person. He would never say anything like that unless he really believed it.

But I couldn't believe it. I had only gotten close to Donna this past year, but my friendship with Roz and Fran went way back. Since we all had boyfriends and went out together, we had gotten even closer. And I felt really close to the other kids in our crowd, too. We hung out together on the park wall or at the ice-cream shop we called "the candy store," on the corner of my block. We went to the movies, concerts, parks, and to the beach together. We had parties or just went up to one another's houses to hang around, talk, and dance. Ever since I had developed a social relationship with boys, the crowd had been the central focus of my life. And now my father was telling me it was just a matter of time before none of us would mean anything to one another. I couldn't believe it, and I let him know why.

He smiled a brief, sad smile. "I can understand why you disagree with me. When I was your age, I had a group of friends I thought I'd be close to forever, too. But it didn't work out that way. As we grew older, we each became involved in what we had to do to make our own lives. We drifted apart and lost contact. Such is the way of the world. I just wanted you to be aware of the fact that it's not good to become dependent on any particular people, places, or things. Nothing stays the same. People change and situations change, and you've got to be flexible enough to change with them."

I thought about what my father had said, but I still couldn't believe it. Just because it had happened to the people he was friendly with when he was young didn't mean the same thing would happen to me.

I knew there were going to be some changes this year. About half the boys in our crowd were starting college, and many of them, like Danny, would be going out of town. Fran had written to me that Danny's possessiveness had become too much for her to stand, and she had decided to break up with him completely. That was one big change. Roz had written that her boyfriend Sheldon's parents had been thinking about moving to the Bronx to be closer to where he was going to college, so that would be another change. But the Bronx was close enough to Washington Heights, the neighborhood in upper Manhattan where we lived, for Sheldon to come around whenever he wanted to, and he and Roz were still going strong. And Donna's boyfriend, Billy, went to Washington, the neighborhood high school where Lenny went, and they were still together. With Lenny and I a couple again, I was sure it was still going to be like old times.

I don't think anyone could have been happier than I was when we started across the George Washington Bridge and saw the massive New York skyline stretching in front of us. I was home. Home to Washington Heights, home to my friends, and best of all, home to Lenny.

It didn't take long after my arrival for him to make his appearance. I had just finished unpacking my suitcase when I heard a familiar whistling coming from the street. I ran to my parents' bedroom, where the windows faced the street. Lenny was standing there looking up at me and grinning.

"So you finally made it back to the city and life once again! Can you come out?"

"Sure! I'll be right down!"

"He's here already? That boyfriend of yours

doesn't even give you time to breathe, does he?" was my mother's remark as I raced by the kitchen, calling to her that I was going out.

There was nothing she could say that could deflate me now. I rushed out of the apartment and practically flew down the first of the three flights of stairs. Lenny met me halfway, and I threw myself into his arms. It was the moment I had been waiting for all summer long.

Just as I thought I would burst from happiness, we were rudely interrupted by teasing voices. "Break it up here! Enough of this already! Let's get moving!"

I looked up to see the laughing faces of two of my best friends, Roz and Donna, accompanied by their boyfriends, Sheldon Emory and Billy Upton.

"Hi guys! Great to see you!" I hugged each of them in turn. It didn't look as if any of them had changed much over the summer. Roz was short, pert, and pretty, with long honey-colored hair and matching eyes. She and Sheldon, who was also short but dark and handsome, made a good-looking pair. Tall, busty Donna's blond hair was bleached even lighter from the sun. She held hands with Billy, who had a hard, thin-lipped, tough-looking face. It was always difficult for me to understand why Donna kept going with Billy, who could be very mean to her, but then again, she never understood why I kept going with Lenny either. Still, most of the time we all got along.

"The only two who are missing now are Fran and Danny," I commented as we all set off walking together toward the park.

"Well, Danny doesn't bother coming all the way from Queens much anymore since Fran broke up with him," Roz explained. "And he's leaving this week for college. But he did say he was going to try to come once more to say good-bye to you, Linda."

"As for Fran, she's too busy with her new social life to come around much," said Donna. "She's met some new boys from other neighborhoods and spends more time with them than she does with us."

"It's no loss either," commented Lenny. "Who needs her around?"

I was surprised at this remark because I had always thought Lenny liked Fran. I didn't have a chance to ask him about it, however, because we arrived at the park wall.

The park was the main gathering place for the teenagers in our neighborhood. Almost four feet high and made of stone, the park wall separated the concrete city neighborhood of brick five- and six-story apartment buildings from the oasis of greenery that was the park. The wall overlooked the baseball field so you could sit up there and watch whatever ballgames were in progress. It was shaded by huge elm trees that provided relief from the summer sun. And it was just a short walk to the candy store on the corner of my block for any necessary refreshments. It was the perfect place to meet and hang out.

When we got to the wall, most of the kids we usually hung out with were already there. I was glad to see them all: tall, gawky Nicky James, who had once had an unreturned crush on me; gorgeous, blond Louie Fields, who I had once been crazy about; busty, big-mouthed Jessie Scaley; sweet, softspoken Kathy Jones; neighborhood muscle man Chris Berland; and others.

Of course, there were people there I was less than overjoyed to see: lover-boy Joel Fudd, who Lenny had been running around with all summer, and some of the girls I knew Lenny had dated. It was hard for me to even look at them although Lenny assured me none of them mattered to him now. I forced myself to go over to them and say hello, and once I saw that nobody had any hard feelings, I felt much better. I didn't like to feel uncomfortable with anyone in the neighborhood.

"Look, there's Danny!" Roz pointed toward the subway entrance, from which Danny's slightly overweight body was emerging. "That shows how important you are, Linda. You can bet Danny came all the way out here just for you."

"Danny!" I went racing up to him and gave him a hug. "I'm so glad you're here!" Danny and I had lived in the same apartment building since I was a little girl. We had grown up together, and I had special feelings for him. I knew Danny would like those special feelings to become romantic ones, but I never could bring myself to feel that way about him. Most of the time he accepted this, but periodically he made some sort of overture toward me to make sure I hadn't changed my mind.

"I came especially to see you," he said after planting a wet kiss on my cheek. "I'm leaving for college the day after tomorrow."

"Wow! It's so hard to believe!" I said. Danny

was only sixteen, but he was such a genius he was already accepted to the Massachusetts Institute of Technology. "But is everything okay? I mean, have you gotten over Fran and all that?"

"Fran? Who can think of Fran when you're around?" He placed his arm around me and gave me a lecherous leer.

"Cut it out, Danny!" I laughingly pulled away from him. "I'm going with Lenny again, you know."

"I know." He wiped a mock tear from his eye. "And you know what a mistake I think that is."

Danny and I walked over to where our crowd was gathered, and I saw that Lenny, as usual, had become the center of attraction. He was telling this story about his mother, and her attempt to cook some fish a neighbor had brought her.

"My mother put some oil in the pan and fried up the fish," I heard him say. "They came out a nice golden brown, but as soon as she took a bite she spit it out and began to shriek, 'I've been poisoned! I've been poisoned!'"

Lenny's face contorted in an imitation of his mother, and his voice became a desperate falsetto. He had a way of telling a story like no one else did. Kids started calling out their encouragement: "What happened next? Go on, Lenny!"

"I was the one who discovered what the problem was. My mother kept the cooking oil on a shelf right next to the cleaning detergent. Instead of adding more oil to the pan, she had poured in Mr. Clean!"

"Oh, no! She didn't!" By the time Lenny finished his story everyone was practically rolling with laughter. "Tell us more, Lenny. Tell us more!" they demanded.

Lenny went on to describe how his mother must have swallowed a gallon of water trying to get the taste out of her mouth. He skillfully mimicked her expressions. I stood next to him the whole time, thinking how glad I was to be Lenny's girlfriend. He was so full of life and had so much personality. There was no one like him—no one.

I was so glad to be together with Lenny, so glad to be back and a part of the crowd again. I put my father's warning completely out of my mind.

Our crowd was special, and nothing would change the good feelings of closeness we had for one another.

Chapter
Five

It was only a few days after my return that Sheldon's parents broke the news to him. They were actually going through with the move they had been considering over the summer. Sheldon's mother had been unhappy living in Washington Heights for some time now. She was unhappy with the bad influence she thought Sheldon's friends had on him; she was unhappy with his hanging around the streets and the poolroom. She had wanted Sheldon to go away to college, but he had refused because he didn't want to leave his friends. She was convinced he wasn't going to make it through college if she didn't get him out of what she considered an undesirable environment. She had found an apartment in the Bronx near where Sheldon would be going to school. Sheldon's family would be moving at the end of the month.

"Oh no!" screamed Roz when Sheldon told us of his plight. "Your parents can't do that!"

"They've already signed the lease," Sheldon said glumly. "I fought with them about it all last night, but they're adamant. They're moving and that's all there is to it! It's like when Danny's parents decided to move to Queens. There was nothing he could do about it either."

"Yeah, and look at what happened to Danny," I said. "He was miserable in Queens. He never made any friends there. He came back to Washington Heights by subway to be with the crowd whenever he could."

"And look at what it did to his relationship with Fran," said Roz. "I bet if Dan hadn't moved away they would still be together today. I don't want anything like that to happen to us, Sheldon. You can't move! We've got to come up with something!"

Leave it to Lenny to come up with an idea. We knew it was a long shot, but it was worth a try. That night we gathered together a bunch of kids from our crowd in front of Sheldon's building and rehearsed a little song Roz and I had written.

They say for every teenage girl and boy
There's just one place that will bring them joy,
And we-ee-ve found ours.
Washington Heights is the place for us
The park, the schoolyard, stores, and bus
We lo-oo-ve it all.
But it's the kids that make it best
If you take Sheldon away we'll never rest
We ne-ee-ed him with us.

Don't go—Please stay. Don't go—Please stay.
PLEASE STAY!

Our goal was to show the Emory family how important it was that Sheldon stay in the neighborhood. We were hoping they would be so moved by our pleas they would back out of the lease.

At exactly seven o'clock, when Sheldon said he would be done with supper, Sheldon's little sister, Sandra, who was too young to hang around with us but didn't want to move from Washington Heights, either, let us in the door. Sheldon had gotten his parents to sit in the living room by telling them he had something important to talk to them about. We could hear him begin his presentation as we tiptoed into the hallway of his apartment.

"Mom and Dad, I don't think you understand how much it means to me to be able to live in Washington Heights. I grew up here. I feel at home here. All my friends are here. They want to let you know how they feel about it, too."

As he said this, Sheldon stepped back into the hallway and signaled us to come into the living room. There were nine of us who filed in, lined up in front of Sheldon's speechless parents, and sang our song. Each one of us had a line to say, and we all joined together for the plea at the end.

I must say we surprised Sheldon's parents. They even looked moved by our pleas to stay. For a moment I thought we might have won. Then Mrs. Emory stood up and began to speak.

"Very cute, boys and girls. We appreciate your efforts and know Sheldon will miss Washington

Heights. But we have very important reasons for leaving. Sheldon must be able to concentrate on his studies now that he's going to college. He cannot do this around some of the bad influences of this neighborhood. We are therefore moving, and that's all there is to it. We've made up our minds.''

When she said this there was a moment of silence. Everyone looked at each other defeatedly. Mrs. Emory had said the same kinds of things I would expect my parents to say under the circumstances. They were always finding things they said I couldn't do because it would interfere with my education. They didn't understand that the resentment I felt at not being allowed to do something I thought was reasonable was more harmful than if they had allowed me to do it. But I had learned that it didn't help to keep arguing with parents when they got stubborn about something, and I certainly wasn't going to continue arguing with Sheldon's. Ready to leave, I started to make my way toward the door. Roz and the other girls in our group followed close behind.

But the boys weren't willing to give up that easily. Apparently, they had come up with a backup plan they hadn't divulged to us girls. Sheldon's mother had a collection of porcelain and glass figurines she had brought from Europe. There was a large one on her coffee table and some smaller ones on her buffet. Before we realized what was happening, Sheldon grabbed the porcelain centerpiece from the table and held it high above him. ''Tell me you're not going to move or I'll smash this to pieces!'' he threatened. ''And my friends will systematically start destroying the others.'' He signaled to the boys, who took positions on either end of the buffet.

We girls froze where we were. We were horrified. I knew the boys' plan would never work. Threats like this would only prove to Sheldon's parents that they were right to get out of the neighborhood. It was the worst thing the boys could have done!

The shrieks that broke out a moment later proved I was right. Sheldon's mother began screaming how if anyone damaged so much as one item in her valuable collection she was going to call the police and have all of us arrested. That was not what I wanted to hear.

''Come on girls—let's get out of here while we still can,'' I urged.

It didn't take much urging. Roz, Donna, and Jessie scrambled out the door after me. We hid in the hallway, waiting to see what would happen to the boys. They came out laughing and joking at how funny it was to see Sheldon's mother so crazy. We girls didn't think it was funny at all.

And the bottom line was that all our efforts hadn't changed anything. By the end of September the Emorys were going to move, and they were taking Sheldon with them.

''It reminds me of when Dan's parents decided to move to Queens, and we were powerless to stop them,'' I told Fran when I finally got to see her the next day. Lenny was busy that afternoon and, for a change, Fran wasn't. We had decided to meet at her house and take a walk to Fort Tryon Park to visit the Cloisters.

The Cloisters is a medieval museum. It has chapels, gardens, and artwork in an atmosphere that makes you feel as if you were actually in a medieval monastery.

I could never get Lenny to go with me to the Cloisters. He said the place gave him the creeps. But Fran and I loved its brooding atmosphere, its long corridors and passageways where you could pretend you were a princess in some faraway place a long-ago time.

We sat now in one of the courtyard gardens, listening to a concert of medieval chamber music. It was very relaxing and very peaceful, and I felt especially close to Fran. Of all my friends, it was she with whom I could have the deepest conversations.

"We tried so hard to convince the Koplers to stay," I recollected. "But nothing would change their minds. And Danny was always miserable after they moved. He never adjusted to living in Queens. He kept coming back to Washington Heights to be with his friends."

"And he always resented his parents for moving," said Fran. "He blamed the move as the reason for our breakup, too."

"Was it?" I asked. "I mean, do you think if he hadn't moved you might still be going together?"

"I don't think so," Fran shook her frizzy head of black hair. "It's true that the move put extra stress on our relationship. It was much harder for us to get together when Dan was so far away. But I'm a believer that true love conquers all. If we were meant to be together, we would have worked it out somehow. We still might, you know. You never can tell what the future has in store. But in the meantime I know I need the freedom to go out with other boys."

"I can understand that. But I still don't see why you had to break up with Danny completely. Didn't you have an agreement where you could each go out with other people if you wanted to?"

"Uh huh." Fran leaned back against a stone pillar and looked up at the clear, late summer sky. "But it wasn't the same. Even though I went out occasionally last year, I still felt I was Dan's girl. I could never really let myself go with other boys because somewhere along the line I would have to answer to Dan. I didn't want to hurt him so I always held myself back. Then I'd get mad at myself for doing that and take it out on him. We'd wind up having one fight after another. The whole situation was no good. I had to break it off to get the freedom I needed."

"So, are you better off this way?"

"I sure am. Oh, I'm not going to tell you I don't miss Dan and the security of knowing I had someone who loved me and of always having a date on Saturday nights. But that wasn't enough for me. There were too many things I had to find out about."

"Things? Like what?"

"Like whether I was attractive to other boys. Whether I could develop relationships with them. What it was like to go out with them and make out with them. And have sex."

"Sex?" I felt my eyes widen. How did Fran mean

52

that? My friends and I had all been brought up by parents with old-fashioned values. They had carefully indoctrinated us about the problems relating to sex: pregnancy, diseases, loss of reputation and self-respect. My friends and I had agreed when we finally did have sex it would be with someone we loved, trusted, and wanted to marry. Of course I knew from my experiences with Lenny how easy it was for one thing to lead to another. But I loved Lenny, and I had been going with him for over a year now. Fran was talking about sex with just anyone as if it were a casual thing. "Just what do you mean by sex?" I asked.

Fran laughed at my expression. "Oh, come on, Linda. Don't be an old prude. I wasn't talking about going 'all the way' with every boy I go out with. But I don't want to feel guilty if we wind up doing some serious making out, either."

"And not going with Danny keeps you from feeling guilty?"

"Correct. Not being labeled 'Danny's girl' makes me free—free to find out what it's like to be with anyone. Be honest, Linda. Didn't you feel freer when you weren't going with Lenny?"

"No. I knew I still cared about him, and that was what mattered. Besides, there wasn't anyone I wanted to make out with, anyway."

Fran shrugged. "Well, I know he did."

"He did what?"

"Feel freer to go out with and make out with girls when he wasn't going with you."

"Oh. And how do you know so much about what Lenny was feeling?" I was suddenly filled with the sick sensation that Fran knew a lot more than she was letting on.

"Because he told me," she answered quickly—too quickly. "Why are you staring at me that way, Linda? Look, everyone knew how Lenny was feeling. When he first broke up with you he was going from one girl to another, going out with and making out with as many as he could. And—well, all right, I'll admit it. I was one of them."

"You? You made out with Lenny?" Even though Fran had just said it to me, I still couldn't believe it was true. "You're one of my best friends, Fran. How could you?"

"Now don't get all excited, Linda. It's no big deal if you think about it, really it isn't. You weren't going with Lenny at the time. The two of you were broken up, remember? That made him fair game as far as I was concerned. I didn't know you were going to get back together—if I had, maybe I would have acted differently. But Lenny's an attractive guy, you know, and he's got a lot of sex appeal. We were sitting on the wall one day, and he said he was thirsty and asked me to walk him to his house to get some juice. There was no one home, and one thing led to another, and there we were making out. It was nothing heavy, just some kissing and minimal petting—no big deal."

"Minimal petting? And what qualifies as minimal petting in your mind?"

"Oh, come on, Linda. You really don't want me to go into exact details, do you?"

"No, I guess not," I sighed. "It's just that the thought of you and Lenny making out is a little hard for me to get used to. Especially since that line about the juice is the same one he used to lure me into his apartment the first time we made out."

"And you probably were just like me. You knew exactly what he was up to, but went along anyway. Believe me, Linda, there was no harm done. It didn't amount to anything, and once the two of you went back together, it stopped completely."

"Gee, I'm so grateful to you for stopping making out with my boyfriend," I said sarcastically.

"Look, Linda. This is the last time I'm going to say this. It's really no big deal. I wouldn't have even told you except I figured it would be better if you heard it from me than someone else. I don't feel as if I've done anything against you, and I still want to be your friend. What do you say?"

What did I say? I leaned back against the pillar nearest me and listened to the music, which, fortunately, was very soothing. The thought of Lenny and Fran making out was painful, but as Fran said, it didn't amount to anything and had stopped when he and I went back together. Fran hadn't done it to hurt me, and she cared enough to be the one to tell me about it, even though it must have been difficult for her to do.

I had been friends with Fran for a long time. I didn't want to lose our friendship over this. It was better to be flexible than to take a stand and make myself unhappy over it.

I would keep my friendship with Fran, although I wasn't sure it could ever be the same. But I was still going to take this up with Lenny!

*   *   *

"Oh, so Fran finally got up the guts to tell you!" Lenny laughed in a way I found infuriating when I confronted him with what Fran had said. We were sitting on the steps between the second and third floor landings in my hallway, a place we often went to talk in private or to make out. "I was wondering if she ever would, the way she was avoiding you when you first came home."

"How come I had to hear it from her?" I demanded angrily. "Why didn't you tell me?"

"I didn't think it would be right for me to say anything. It would be talking behind her back, ruining her reputation. So I left it up to her. I'm glad she told you, because it wouldn't have been good if you had found out from someone else, even though the whole thing was no big deal."

"No big deal? That's the same thing Fran kept saying. What did you two do, agree upon the terms you would use and everything?" The thought of Fran and Lenny plotting what they would tell me was making me feel sick.

"Linda! You're letting your emotions get the best of you!" Lenny laughed again, but stopped when he saw the look on my face. "Look, baby, I want you to understand something. I went out with quite a few girls while you were away, and I made out with even more. I could make you a list of them, but I don't think that would be beneficial to either of us. It was something I had to get out of my system, and I did it. It was no big deal because none of those girls mattered. When I realized that, I came back to you. That stuff was all in the past.

We've got the future, and that's what counts. Isn't it?'' He reached for my hand when he said this.

His touch sent shivers through my body. It never ceased to amaze me, the effect Lenny had on me. I was furious when I first confronted him. A few words and a few touches later and he had me practically eating out of his hand.

I smiled weakly. He put his arm around me, and I snuggled up against him. ''Okay, I'll consider that stuff all in the past,'' I said. ''If you'll tell me one thing.''

''What's that?''

''Did Fran make out better than I do?'' I knew it was wrong to ask that question, but something inside me just had to know.

''Of course not,'' he laughed. ''No one makes out better than you—that's why I keep coming back for more!''

He kissed me when he said that, and it was wonderful. But deep inside I still felt this uneasiness whenever I thought about the summer.

I was glad the summer was behind me now. In fact, in a strange way I was almost looking forward to the start of school.

Chapter

Six

*E*ven though part of me had been looking forward to it, I felt very alone the first day of school. Lenny and most of my friends went to our neighborhood high school, Washington. I didn't, however; I went to the Bronx High School of Technology, a special school which accepted students only after they had passed an entrance exam.

Originally, I had applied for Tech because Louie went there, and at the time I was crazy over Louie. But now that Louie had graduated, I didn't even have him as a schoolmate. No one else I was friendly with in the neighborhood went to Tech. I was all alone as I stood on the subway platform waiting for the first of two trains that would take me there.

I guess I was lucky; getting good grades in school always came easily to me. I learned early there were little tricks that helped me to do well. The first was to pay attention; teachers almost always stated exactly what they expected you to know if you listened. The second was to take good notes and go over them as often as possible at odd moments like riding on the train or while eating lunch. The repetition helped me remember what I had studied, and I never had to panic and cram before a big exam. This system worked for me, and I got good grades, which was essential while living with my parents, who thought education was the most important thing in the world.

Unfortunately, my doing well in school created some problems in my relationship with Lenny, who was not a good student. In fact, on his last report card, he had failed every subject.

This wasn't because Lenny was stupid; if anything, he was one of the brightest kids in our neighborhood. He had done well in school when he was younger and could get by on brains alone. He had even passed the test for a special high school, but his mother hadn't let him go because she thought the trip was too far for him to make each day.

Lenny had gone to Washington, and that's when his troubles started. He was having a lot of problems at home. His parents were always fighting; then his father moved out and Lenny's mother fought with him. With all that was going on at home, he found it increasingly difficult to concentrate in school. He claimed the subjects he was taking were irrelevant and his teachers were boring. He began to cut classes and to fall behind in his work. The more he did this, the harder it became for him to keep going to classes. He wound up cutting so many that he was automatically failed.

This was hard for me to accept. In my house it was taken for granted my brothers and I would do well in school. I couldn't imagine how Lenny, who was so bright, could allow his whole life to be ruined by failing in school. I tried my hardest to help him study. I begged him not to cut classes and kept nagging him to go to school each day. Nothing worked, and we had a lot of fights because of the situation.

This year, Lenny promised things would be different. "It's a brand new year, and I've got a chance for a brand new start. I'm going to all my classes from the very first day."

I was glad to hear him say that. But I also felt a little sad about it. Last year, Lenny and Billy had cut the first day of school and come out to Tech with me. I had felt so wonderful having Lenny with me and had fantasized how fantastic it would be to go to school together with him every day. I longed to have him keep me company this first day of school as well, but I knew it was more important that he start the school year off the right way.

So I got on the train by myself. I had brought along a book to make the ride go faster. I became so engrossed in it that I didn't even notice who else was on the train until someone plopped down in the seat next to mine.

"Hi, Linda! Ready to get back to the old grind?"

I looked up. It was Cesca Ondell, a girl who had been in my math class last year. Cesca was generally regarded as somewhat weird, but I liked her.

She was tall, with straight, long dark hair, and a slightly oriental cast to her features.

"Oh, hi, Cesca. As ready as I'll ever be. What about you?"

"I'm actually looking forward to it. I had a pretty boring summer, and there are things I like about school. Like the Volleyball Club."

"Volleyball Club? I didn't even known there was such a thing at Tech."

"There is. We get together every Wednesday afternoon and practice, and we'll have tournaments at the end of the year. But it's mostly for fun and for exercise. You ought to join, Linda."

"Well, I don't know," I said reluctantly. "Most of the time I like to go straight home from school to see my boyfriend, Lenny."

"Lenny? Isn't that the same boy who broke up with you at the end of last semester?"

"Uh huh. But I went back with him again over the summer."

"Well, that just goes to show you, you can't count on a boy to always be there for you. What if he drops you again? Don't put all your eggs in one basket, as the old saying goes. Get some balance in your life. Come join the Volleyball Club, it'll be good for you."

"I'll think about it," I promised. I knew Cesca was right. Putting my eggs in one basket with Lenny was a mistake I had made before and been sorry for. But the part of me that was so attracted to Lenny wanted to spend every minute I possibly could with him. That part didn't want to bother with clubs.

I was glad to find that Cesca was not only in my math and gym classes this year, but in science class as well. Not only that, we shared the same lunch period and could eat together.

Although this was my second year at Tech, I still didn't feel as if I belonged there. I guess most of the reason for this was my own fault. Because my life revolved so much around Lenny and the kids in my neighborhood, I didn't make much effort to get to know the kids at my school. But part of the reason was that my schedule was so messed up, and that wasn't my fault at all.

I had come to Tech with advanced placement in most of my subjects. As a result, although I was officially in tenth grade this year, I took math, science, history, and Spanish with the eleventh graders. The rest of the kids in my homeroom took their classes together, so I didn't fit in with them. The kids in my eleventh grade classes knew I belonged in tenth grade, so I didn't fit in with them either.

That's why I was so grateful to find someone like Cesca, who accepted me for what I was without worrying about where I fit in.

"How's this table?" I asked, pointing to one near a window where we could look out on a bit of grass and a patch of sky.

"Great—I hate being cooped up in this building all day. It makes me feel freer to be able to at least look outside," said Cesca, as she pulled a brown paper bag out of her purse.

"I'm glad to see someone else 'brown bagging' it for lunch," I said as I pulled out my own lunch bag.

"I decided taking lunch from home might be a good way to lose a few pounds. The cafeteria lunches are loaded with calories."

"Oh, I don't see why you have to worry about your weight, Linda." Cesca bit into a sandwich that looked and smelled like tuna. "I bring my lunch because I think the cafeteria food tastes horrendous!"

"It does," I giggled. "But didn't you ever notice how the other kids look at you strangely when you bring a bag lunch?"

"If they do that's their problem," Cesca shrugged. "I can't be bothered with worrying about what other people might think about what I'm doing."

"You're right. It really doesn't matter," I agreed. I was pleased that Cesca was the kind of person who thought for herself. Most of the time I did, too, and it was good to get some reinforcement.

"Are you saving those seats for anyone?" A boy's voice interrupted us. I looked up and saw Sandy and Mike, two boys from our math class.

"Nope. You guys can sit here if you like," Cesca answered.

I smiled at them, a bit uncomfortably. Last year, Sandy had acted as if he liked me. When he had found out I had broken up with Lenny, he had asked me to a few school dances, and we had spent some time studying together. I liked Sandy; he was nice and very smart, but I liked him only as a friend. I was hoping that over the summer he might have come to like me as a friend as well.

Sandy sat next to me and Mike sat next to Cesca.

Sandy ignored his lunch and gazed right into my eyes. "So tell me about your summer, Linda. What's new with you?"

I squirmed. I could tell already that Sandy still liked me, and not as a friend. I hated to be in that position! What do you say to let a boy know you don't like him the way he likes you without hurting his feelings? I had never been good at handling this type of situation.

"Oh, not much happened over the summer. I was away in the country working as a counselor, and now I'm back again."

"And she's back with her boyfriend, too," Cesca chimed in.

I threw her a dirty look, as I knew this wasn't what Sandy wanted to hear. But on second thought, maybe it was good that Cesca said that. The truth would keep him from getting up any false hopes.

"Boyfriend? Is that the same one you were going with last year?" asked Mike. "The one who kept breaking up with you and going with you again?"

I felt myself blushing. "Yeah, that's the one."

"Well, you must be some kind of masochist or something," said Mike. "I don't know what you want with a guy like that when there are plenty of nice ones around who would treat you right if you gave them the chance."

Mike didn't look at Sandy when he said this, but I knew perfectly well he was talking about him. And Mike was probably right. Sandy would treat me better than Lenny did if I gave him the chance. But the fact remained I felt nothing when I was with

Sandy, and the very thought of Lenny sent my heart beating wildly.

Even now, as I thought of him, I was filled with longing to be with him. Everything else—lunch, finding out about the rest of my teachers or the kids who were going to be in my classes, Sandy, Mike, and Cesca—faded into the background. I couldn't wait to get home and find out how Lenny had made out the first day of school!

Kids from our crowd were already hanging around the candy store by my corner when I finally arrived home that afternoon. Everyone was comparing notes on the classes and teachers they had this year.

Lenny wasn't there yet, and I stood on the outskirts of the conversation, feeling somewhat left out. Except for Roz, who went to a special school called Fine Arts, the other girls in the neighborhood all went to Washington. All the boys who were still in high school went there, too. They got to ride to school together on the bus, eat lunch together, and have classes together. I couldn't identify with their experiences at all.

I was glad when Roz finally showed up. At least she was a fellow outcast. "Hi Roz! How was your first day?" I asked as she approached.

"Fantastic!" she bubbled. "You wouldn't believe the great classes I have this year. I've got a design class given by a professional clothing designer, and an art history class that includes trips to all the major museums."

"That does sound great!" Art was something I

could relate to since I was good in art myself. But I thought of art as a hobby, not as something I wanted to make my career the way Roz did.

"But the classes aren't as great as some of the boys who are in them," Roz said with a laugh. "There's this guy, Marty, in art history, who's simply awesome! You should see him—he's tall and has green eyes, and this unruly mop of dark, curly hair!"

"Hang on a minute there, Roz. Are you forgetting you're going with Sheldon?"

"No, of course not." Roz let out a sigh. "But truthfully, Linda, when I'm with some of the boys from school it sometimes makes me wonder why I am going with Sheldon. I really have much more in common with them; they're much more cultural. Sheldon doesn't know the difference between Rembrandt and Picasso. He refuses to even come with me to a museum or a play, where he might be exposed to a little culture. As much as I care for him, when I'm with someone like Marty, I totally forget about Sheldon. Doesn't that happen to you when you're with someone really great from school?"

"Who me?" I looked at Roz to see if she was serious. When I saw she was, I shook my head. "Not at all. There's no one at Tech who interests me. I spend my time at school counting the minutes until I can come home to Lenny."

"You're hopeless, Linda." Roz frowned. "It's not healthy to be so involved with anyone, especially someone like Lenny, who keeps changing his mind about how he feels about you. How come he's not even here now to see you?"

"I don't know. Everyone else from Washington has been home awhile, but no one seems to know what happened to him. Wait, isn't that Lenny coming from the bus stop now?" I pointed up the block to where I could make out his tall frame and bouncy walk even from a distance. But Lenny was not walking alone, and I couldn't make out who the short, female person was walking with him.

"It's Fran!" Roz recognized her before I did. I felt my stomach clutch at her name. It was bad enough that Lenny was late coming from school. What was he doing with Fran?

It didn't take me long to find out. Fran spouted the news as if it were something I should actually be happy about. "Here I was, looking for a sport to join now that I'm going to Washington, and not having the slightest idea of which one to go for. Then Lenny comes along with the perfect answer—the bowling team."

"Bowling?" I repeated dumbly.

"Sure," Fran chattered away. "It's good exercise, but not strenuous, and I've gotten rather good at bowling. Not only that, it's one of the few school teams that are coeducational. Lenny and I are going to be on the team together!" She smiled and turned to Lenny. "Remember, practice is every Wednesday. So be sure to get your schedule in order and keep those grades up now. The whole team is counting on you!"

She glanced at her watch and continued her monologue. "Darn! I didn't realize how late tryouts would end. I promised my neighbor I'd babysit this afternoon, and I'm practically late already. Got to run. So long, everyone. I'll see you in school tomorrow, Lenny, and we'll discuss the team some more. Ciao!''

"Ciao?" I repeated as I watched her disappear down the block.

"It's an Italian way of saying good-bye," said Lenny. "Fran picked it up this summer. She thinks it makes her sound cool."

"Oh? And is during the summer when you two decided to join the bowling team together?" I struggled to keep back the anger and jealousy that rose at the thought of Lenny and Fran together during the summer.

"That's not what happened at all," he insisted. "You heard Fran say that we just made up our minds to try out for the team today."

"Oh? Just like that?"

"Yup. Just like that." Lenny laughed, which only made me angrier. "Now look, Linda, you know I was always good at bowling. I thought about getting on the team last year, but never bothered. You have to maintain a 'C' average to stay on the team, so they're only letting me in on a probationary basis and only because I'm such a great bowler. I thought maybe being on the team would give me some motivation to do better in school, so I signed up for it. When I ran into Fran in the cafeteria and told her about it, she decided to try out, too. It's as simple as that!"

I felt my anger dissipate as Lenny said this to me.

Somehow, no matter what he did, he had a way of explaining it so I couldn't stay mad at him.

The anger left, but the jealousy didn't. I still wasn't happy about the idea of having Lenny and Fran thrown together regularly for any reason. It was too easy for them to wind up replaying the kind of scene that went on this summer when I was away.

But Lenny was entitled to be on the bowling team if he wanted—I had no right to stop him. And I certainly couldn't do anything to stop Fran. I would just have to hope that there really was nothing going on between them and resign myself to Wednesday afternoons without him.

Wednesday afternoons. I was sure that was the day Cesca had told me the Volleyball Club met after school. I forced my face into what I hoped was a natural-looking smile.

"Well, that's fine with me, Lenny, because it so happens I'm joining a club that practices on Wednesdays, too—the Volleyball Club!"

"You are?" He looked at me in surprise. "How come? I mean—you didn't know I was going to be busy on Wednesdays or anything."

"No. I just decided on my own. After all, Lenny, no one should put all their eggs in one basket. There has to be a balance in life, and it's probably good for us to do these things on our own."

"Any boys in the Volleyball Club?" asked Roz, who had been listening to our conversation with an expression of amusement.

"Not on the team, but I understand they do come to cheer us on when we have our tournaments," I answered. I was delighted to detect a look of jealousy flicker across Lenny's face.

Of course I knew there was nothing for him to be jealous about. There wasn't one boy who interested me in the entire Bronx High School of Technology.

But I didn't have to let him know that. Cesca was right. I really did need to have more balance in my life. And balance was hard to come by when I was so absolutely crazy over Lenny.

Chapter
Seven

As we settled into the routines of the new school year, I couldn't help but notice that there were subtle changes going on in our crowd, much as my father had predicted. Most of them were changes I didn't care for.

It's not that the changes were anyone's fault. They were merely a result of the fact that we were all a year older and therefore at different stages of our lives. Some of the boys, like Danny, had gone away to college. Others, like Louie, had stayed home but were now busy with college work and activities. They didn't have as much time to hang out and come to get-togethers on the weekends.

The girls were changing, too. They had all started high school and were meeting kids from other neighborhoods. Some had hooked up with other friends and crowds, and others, like Roz, hung on to our

crowd but brought in new ideas that were sometimes disturbing.

But what affected me most were the changes in
the couples I was closest to. Since Danny and Fran
were broken up completely, of course they weren't
a couple at all anymore. And once Sheldon moved
he rarely came around during the week, so Roz
busied herself more frequently with kids and events
in her school. As for Donna and Billy, they had so
many fights that they seemed to be breaking up
more than going together. Each time she broke up
with Billy, Donna seemed to get more friendly with
the girls who went to school with her at Washington, and less friendly with Roz and me.

So, even though we still gathered at the park wall
whenever possible, our crowd was not what it used
to be. Everyone seemed to be pulled in different
directions. There weren't as many parties to go to
or couples to go out with on weekends. Sometimes
I liked going out alone with Lenny and spending
time with only him. But sometimes I missed the fun
we had with other couples.

That's why I was so happy to hear that Joel Fudd,
one of the neighborhood's most hopeless flirts, had
settled down with one girlfriend. Joel was very
handsome. He was well built and had brown eyes
and hair that curled around an adorable baby face.
But Joel was as conceited as they come. Priding
himself on his "love them and leave them" attitude,
he left a string of broken hearts wherever he went.

It was while he was broken up with me over the
summer that Lenny became very friendly with Joel.
This friendship made me uneasy because Joel would

always make remarks about how terrible it was for Lenny to be tied down to one girl and how he should be spending less time with me and more time out with the boys. It was a big relief to me that Joel finally had a girlfriend of his own.

The girl was Penny Weiner, and she had been after Joel for a long time. Penny was a pretty, fun-loving girl, short and dark with big brown eyes and thick brown hair. For a while she had been friendly with Renee Berkley, who was a big flirt and had earned herself a reputation for being fast, but their friendship had ended when Renee began hanging around with a tough crowd that was known to be using drugs.

"Watching what drugs were doing to those kids convinced me I didn't want any part of that scene," Penny confided in me one day. "You could actually see them go downhill. One day they were doing okay in school; the next they were flunking out. They began getting into trouble with the police and messing up their bodies, too. One look at them and I knew that drugs weren't for me."

I was glad to hear Penny say this. I didn't have to be around kids who took drugs to know they weren't for me. The stuff I read in the papers and the things I was learning this year in health class in school were enough to convince me to stay away from drugs and from people who used them. I wasn't interested in drinking, either.

That's why I was surprised when Lenny told me that Joel and Penny had gone drinking together one Saturday night and were inviting us to join them the following weekend to finish off the bottle. Now I was aware that almost all the boys in our crowd had tried drinking. I didn't like it, especially when Lenny was with them, but they had never brought alcohol to parties and didn't do it when the girls were around, so it had never directly affected me. This was the first I'd heard of any of my close friends taking part, and it made me uncomfortable.

"I really didn't want to drink when Joel first brought it up, either," Penny admitted when I questioned her the next afternoon.

"So, why did you?"

"Joel wanted me to. He said it would be fun. And you know how Joel is—a real run-around. I'm never sure of how to keep him interested, so I try to do whatever might make him happy. I thought drinking with him might bring us closer together."

"Did it?"

Penny looked thoughtful. "Well, not really. But Joel did stay with me later than usual that night. And when he left me he went straight home instead of bumming around with the boys the way he usually does. So maybe it was good for our relationship."

"Well, I don't see where drinking could possibly help my relationship with Lenny," I said. "And truthfully, I can't stand the way the stuff tastes. My parents never really drink at home, but once my father had company and served some scotch and soda. I accidentally took a sip from his glass, not knowing there was liquor in it. It was awful! It burned my throat, and I choked so badly I had to run to spit it out in the sink and gulp down glass after glass of water.''

"That's because the first taste is the worst," said Penny. "By the second drink, it doesn't taste so bad at all."

"Great," I said grimly. "So if you can make it past the first one, maybe you can tolerate the second. It still doesn't make sense to me why people bother with that stuff."

"Aw, come on, Linda," Penny laughed gaily. "At least come out with us on Saturday night. No one's going to force you to drink if you don't want to, and we'll have a good time. You ought to have more fun in your life. You're much too serious, you know."

If Penny could have picked one thing to say to convince me to come with them Saturday night, it was that I was too serious. It was the same thing that Lenny was always telling me, and I knew he was right. Things would be a lot easier for me if I stopped analyzing everything and brooding over each decision as if it were a major turning point in my life.

I guess the reason I tended to be that way was because I could also be very compulsive. There were plenty of times when I lost my cool and acted on raw emotion without taking time to stop, think, and control myself. Most of the time, those situations wound up disastrously. I would open my big mouth and say or do something that would get me into trouble.

As I got older, I tried hard to avoid getting into

"out of control" situations. As a result, I sometimes gave the impression of being too serious.

That really wasn't the way I wanted to be. I did
love to have fun. That was probably one of the main
reasons I was so attracted to Lenny—he injected
fun into everything we did. But Lenny also tended
to get carried away with whatever he was doing and
lose control. Sometimes that made me tighten up
even more, as if I needed to have enough control
for both of us.

At any rate, I was determined to show everyone
I could have as much fun as they could. Penny and
Joel called for me, and we walked together to Lenny's apartment, where we were to have our own
private "party." Lenny's mother was out, so we
had the place to ourselves.

"Welcome to my humble abode!" Lenny bowed
with mock formality as he opened the front door.
He led us to his room, which I noticed he had at
least made an attempt to straighten. The usual state
of Lenny's room was one of complete disarray—
the bed unmade, and food, clothes, books, news-
papers, and records strewn all over. Not only that,
but the one window faced the wall of an alleyway,
not three feet away, making the room dark and
dreary inside even on the brightest of days.

But now, at night, you couldn't see outside anyway. And Lenny had put out some pretzels and
potato chips and soda, as if this were a real party.
He put on some records, and we started to dance.
There were no signs of alcohol, so I began to relax
and enjoy myself.

How I loved to dance with Lenny. Even though I

was only five feet tall and he, at close to six feet, towered over me, I felt as if I were floating in heaven when he took me in his arms. I would rest my head on his shoulder, inhale the delicious mixture of shaving cream, hair spray, or whatever he had on, and get lost in the sensation of feeling our bodies swaying in rhythm to the music. Sometimes we would start to kiss right there in the middle of a dance. It was wonderful!

We had settled into our normal routine and were standing there kissing to the music, when Joe interrupted us. "Hey, you two. Don't get so carried away that you forget I brought my friend, Mr. Wilson, here to share with you."

What Joel referred to as "Mr. Wilson," was really a bottle of some sort of liquor, which he proceeded to pour into our glasses of soda. "Don't put any in mine," I said quickly. Then I added, "I mean I've already tasted liquor mixed with soda, and I don't like it that way."

Joel shrugged. "If you ask me, it's a lot worse to drink Mr. Wilson straight. But suit yourself, Linda. You always had some strange tastes. Why else would you pick Lenny?" He laughed, guzzled down his drink, then laughed some more as if this were really funny.

Something about this whole situation was scary to me. I held on to Lenny, hoping to keep dancing and keep him away from the liquor at the same time. But when the record ended, he lost no time drinking down what Joel had poured in his glass. His face didn't look as if he were enjoying the taste, but he immediately asked Joel for a refill.

Joel was glad to oblige. He, Penny, and Lenny all managed to keep drinking the stuff despite occasional coughing and choking.

I felt very much the outsider as I watched them. We had all been having a great time before the arrival of Mr. Wilson. I didn't see what alcohol could do to make things better.

Joel put on a fast record, and he and Penny began dancing wildly to the music. "Come on, Linda. Let's dance, too," Lenny surprised me by saying. He never liked to dance fast dances; he claimed he didn't know how to stay in step. But drinking seemed to make him lose these inhibitions. He gyrated around the room as if he were king of the dance floor.

I joined him, and the four of us danced around, bumping into each other, singing along with the music, laughing, and having a good time. By the time the dance was over, we were all out of breath. And thirsty. Lenny poured some more soda, and Joel began pouring Mr. Wilson. Away went my good feelings, and back came the uncomfortable ones.

"How about trying some, Linda?" said Joel. "I'll put in just a little so you won't even taste it."

"Come on, Linda. Nothing horrible is going to happen," urged Penny.

"Sure it will. At midnight she'll turn into a pumpkin," joked Lenny.

I looked from Joel to Penny to Lenny and squirmed. They weren't really putting heavy pressure on me, but I felt pressured just the same. If I didn't drink, I would be an outsider at this party all night long. Everyone would think I was some sort of prude.

"Okay. Just a little," I agreed.

"Great! Mr. Wilson will be so-oo happy!" Joel poured what seemed to be a small amount into my glass.

Little as it was, it was enough to ruin the taste of my soda. "Yuck! This is horrible!" I screwed up my face in distaste.

"Remember what I said about how it gets better after the first one," laughed Penny, polishing off her drink.

I tried another sip. "It doesn't taste any better," I reported.

"I said the next drink tastes better, not the next sip, silly! You've got to drink the whole glass before you can expect to feel any different."

I looked at my drink and frowned. There was no way I was going to get down a whole glass of that stuff. But now that I had begun to drink, I was suddenly filled with curiosity about what it would feel like to get drunk.

I figured there was only one way to find out. I might not be able to drink glasses of the foul-tasting liquid, but if I didn't mix it with soda, I'd only have to get down a smaller amount. I thought of how I used to take medicine I hated when I was a little kid. I would hold my nose, swallow it real fast, then wash it down with a glass of water. Maybe the same process would work now.

"Here, you finish this." I poured what was left of my drink into Lenny's glass and filled mine with plain soda. "You guys can waste time with mixed drinks if you want to. I'd rather take mine straight!"

Before I could change my mind or anyone could stop me, I held my nose with one hand, grabbing the bottle of Mr. Wilson with the other, and started chugging it down as fast as I could. It burned my throat like crazy, but I swallowed it anyway.

"Hey, Linda. Cut it out—you've had enough!" It was Lenny's voice that finally stopped me. He grabbed my hand and made me put the bottle down. "This is your first time. You don't want to get sick or anything."

"I'm okay," I said, gasping for breath. I could feel the alcohol burning my insides, and I quickly guzzled down the soda I had poured to cool my throat. I looked around and saw everyone staring at me in amazement. Suddenly, their expressions struck me as very funny, and I began to laugh.

"Ha-ha-ha! Look at you guys! Ha-ha! You look as if you've never seen anyone take a drink before. And you're supposed to be the ones who are experienced. Ha-ha-ha-ha-ha!"

I kept laughing as if I had told the funniest joke ever. Then Penny started laughing, and Joel and Lenny joined in. We laughed so hard that Penny had to go racing to the bathroom. That set everyone off laughing again.

Joel, Lenny, and I plopped down on the floor, holding our stomachs and rolling about. We still hadn't recovered when Penny came back. "Come on, everyone, let's dance some more." She put on another fast record and pulled Joel to his feet.

Lenny stood up next and grabbed my hand to

help me to my feet. I got up there, but I found I couldn't stay there. There was something wrong with the room. It kept spinning around my head. Not only that, but Lenny, Joel, and Penny were spinning around me, too.

I tried taking a step and found myself collapsing to the floor again. "Every-everything's going round and round," I murmured. I sprawled on the floor and started to laugh again as Lenny's face came into focus above me. He looked worried, and I couldn't understand why.

"Linda, are you okay?"

"Sure I'm okay, whad'ya think?" I giggled. "I just like it down here on the floor in the middle of ev'thing."

"Fine. But I want you to get up now. Penny's going to put on a slow record, and we'll dance to that."

" 'Kay," I said agreeably. I allowed Lenny to pull me to my feet again. I leaned against him for support as he led me around the floor. "See, I can stand up just fine!" I flashed him my brightest smile, but as I did that the room began spinning worse than ever. Lenny's face was lost in a blur of colors that whirled round and round.

And what was that song Penny had put on? Lenny had said it was supposed to be a slow dance. Then why was that music throbbing in my ears so loudly that I thought my head was going to burst? "Stop it! Stop that noise!" I shouted. "Turn that record off!"

I guess someone did because the music stopped, and I was surrounded by silence. But for some reason the silence was every bit as loud and painful as the music had been. It seemed to be closing in on me, and I put my hands over my ears to shut it out. I closed my eyes, trying to stop the room from spinning, but the spinning continued within my head. I couldn't stand the way I felt!

What was wrong with me? Could I have gotten drunk from the alcohol? It didn't seem like I had taken so much, but it was hard to tell when I had gulped it down that way. Everyone had said drinking was supposed to be fun and make you feel good, but good was the last word you could use to describe this feeling!

It was awful. There was a pounding pressure in my head that built up until I thought I was going to explode. And then I got a nauseous feeling in my stomach, and I knew I was going to be very, very sick.

I didn't remember much of what happened after that, just bits and pieces of horrible scenes as if from a nightmare. I remembered being in Lenny's bathroom staring down the toilet bowl at my own vomit while someone held my head. I remembered fighting Penny as she tried to force me to drink black coffee. I remembered drinking some and feeling sicker still. I remembered Lenny pushing us out the door to his apartment, saying we had to leave before his mother came home and found us this way. I remembered not caring how she found me, because all I wanted was to lie right down there and die. I remembered going out in the street and being sick again, leaning over the gutter and heaving until there was nothing left inside of me to throw up.

I remembered staring at the door to my apartment as Lenny inserted the key for me, filled with horrible fear that my parents might still be awake to see me in the condition I was in. They would absolutely kill me if they found me drunk; I knew it.

I struggled to pull myself together. I tried to force my brain to concentrate on what I was doing so I could look and act and talk as normally as possible.

The door opened. Lenny handed me the key. That was the last thing I remembered!

Chapter
Eight

I woke up the next morning in my own bed, feeling sick as could be. My head ached; my throat was sore; my stomach was still queasy. My mouth was dry, and the taste of alcohol and stale vomit lingered.

For a moment I didn't understand what was wrong with me, but that horrible taste of alcohol brought it all back: the nightmare that last evening had turned into, the jumble of scenes that replayed in my mind, getting drunk and getting sick. It had to be one of the worst experiences I had ever had in my life.

I forced myself to sit up in bed. I swung my feet to the floor, then pushed myself up to standing. My legs felt like lead, but at least they held me up, and I was able to stagger over to the bathroom.

I turned on the shower full blast and stayed under

there a long time, as if the stream of water could somehow cleanse away the dirty feelings I had over what had happened last night. I furiously rubbed myself dry with my towel and stood staring at myself in the mirror.

I looked awful. My face, even after the shower, was tinted green, and my eyes were red. But at least the room wasn't spinning anymore, and I felt stronger on my feet. I brushed my teeth and rinsed my mouth with mouthwash three times in an attempt to get rid of the awful taste. It was only then that I felt equipped to go out and face my parents. I forced myself to smile as I walked into the kitchen, where they were finishing breakfast, and said, "Good morning."

"You slept awfully late this morning," my mother commented.

"That's because she was out so late last night," said my father.

"That's right. She was out awfully late," my mother agreed. "I was going to speak to you about it last night, Linda, but truthfully, I was too tired to get out of bed. I don't mind if there's a party or special event going on and you arrange to be out later, but on an ordinary Saturday night you don't have to be out so late. It must have been practically midnight when you got in last night."

"Eleven fifty-seven, exactly. I looked at the clock," said my father.

Ordinarily, this conversation would have been very upsetting to me. I had fought long and hard to have my parents lift the ridiculous curfews they had placed on me. Until recently, I had to be home by nine on weeknights and eleven on weekends, unless there was a special event that ended later. This year, my parents agreed to reduce these times to "guidelines"—times I knew they would like to have me home by, but I was allowed to be home later, so long as it was reasonable.

I didn't think eleven fifty-seven was unreasonable for a Saturday night; ordinarily, I would have argued the point. But today I was so grateful to find out my parents had been in bed and hadn't seen me when I got home last night that I would have gone along with anything. "Was it that late? Sorry, I didn't realize. I'll pay more attention next time I go out."

"And tell your boyfriend he should pay attention to the time, too," Mom had to throw in. "If he cared about you he'd be concerned about when he brought you home. Sleep is essential for your health, you know."

"I know, Ma." I poured myself some orange juice and sat down at the table. I didn't want to argue the point that if people stayed out late on Saturday night there was nothing wrong with sleeping late on Sunday to make up for it. My parents regarded any kind of excess as practically sinful, and staying out late fell into this category.

The orange juice did not sit well in my stomach, and I realized there was no way I could finish drinking it without getting sick all over again. I couldn't spill it out, either. My mother was watching me carefully, as always, monitoring my food intake. The only way I could see out of being forced to eat breakfast was to arrange to have an accident.

"I guess I'll have some cereal." I reached for the box that was sitting in the middle of the table. As I did so my elbow banged into the glass of juice, knocking it over.

"Linda! You clumsy thing!" My mother hated to see things spill. "There's juice running all over! Quick! Get the sponge and wipe it up before it ruins the rest of the food!"

I sopped up the spreading river of juice while Mom pulled things off the table. Just as I had hoped, she was upset enough to forget about food for a moment.

It was only when I had helped clean up the kitchen and was ready to go outside that my mother remembered I hadn't eaten. "Linda! You didn't have breakfast! You can't go out without nourishment!"

"Oh, I'm not very hungry this morning, Ma. I'll butter up a roll and take it with me."

"Teenagers. I don't know how they survive on what they eat," I heard my mother grumble to my father.

I drew a sigh of relief as I made it out the door. I had gotten past the first obstacle—my parents hadn't found out about last night. But now I had to face Penny, Joel, and Lenny. I didn't know what kinds of crazy things I might have said or done that I'd have to live down, or even if they'd want to have anything to do with me again.

Fortunately, neither Joel, Penny, nor Lenny held my dumb actions against me. In fact, they seemed to feel guilty for having been the ones to try to convince me to drink in the first place.

"I should have known drinking wasn't for you," Lenny told me as the four of us sat on the park wall discussing what had happened. "Of course I didn't expect you to guzzle down the amount you did, but I shouldn't have tried to pressure you to drink at all."

"No, you shouldn't have," I agreed. "No one should pressure anyone else to do something they really don't want to do. But that's really beside the point, which is that I knew drinking wasn't for me, and I didn't stick to what I knew was right. I can't blame anyone but myself."

"Well, there was no way of telling how it was going to turn out," said Penny. "You really couldn't know drinking was wrong for you until you tried it."

"Oh yes I could," I insisted. "I don't have to rob or murder someone to know that it's wrong for me, do I?"

"Oh, come on, Linda. That's ridiculous," said Joel. "You can't consider robbing and murdering, which everyone knows are wrong, in the same category as drinking."

"No-oo," I said slowly, trying to come up with the words to explain what I meant. "I guess robbery and murder weren't the best examples, because it's obvious those things are wrong. I'm talking about the smaller things, those times when it's hard to decide what you should or shouldn't do in a situation."

"What about them?" asked Lenny.

"Well, sometimes when I'm faced with making a decision, there's a part of me that tries to convince me it's okay to do a certain thing I really know is wrong for me. But then there's another part of me, almost like a little voice, that tells me what I know is right. As long as I listen to that little voice, I find I don't regret it."

"Then how come you're always making so many dumb mistakes?" challenged Joel.

"Because I don't always want to listen. That little voice always seems to speak in a whisper. And then there's that other part of me—the part that was so anxious to see what it was like to be drunk that it didn't even care if I got sick. That part shouts at me so loudly I sometimes forget to listen for the whispering voice at all."

"Is she crazy, or is she crazy?" Joel looked at Lenny and laughed.

But Lenny wasn't laughing. "No. Actually, what she says makes sense, Joel. When I think about it, I've had that experience sometimes myself, when I've gone ahead and done something I wanted to do but knew inside wasn't right for me. It always caused me grief in the long run, but I went ahead and did it just the same. I wonder why that is?"

"Maybe we learn better when we do it the hard way," I said. "A painful lesson is harder to forget."

"Like the one you learned last night," laughed Penny. "I bet you won't do anything like that again, will you?"

"Nope." I shook my head emphatically. "Just

the thought of anything alcoholic makes my stomach turn.''

It was several weeks after this, when I had begun to believe that all connections between myself and alcohol were well behind me, that Lenny's uncle Art appeared on the scene. Uncle Art was an alcoholic, although he claimed to be reformed, clean, and sober when he showed up at Lenny's door. He begged Mrs. Lipoff to let him stay there until he could find a place for himself. He had decided to move back to New York from California, where he'd been living, but he was a little short of funds for the moment.

The immediate effect Uncle Art's arrival had on me was a negative one. Instead of coming around and seeing me after school the way he usually did, Lenny began going home to spend some time with his uncle. According to Lenny, Art told some fascinating stories.

"You've got to meet my uncle," Lenny said to me when I finally saw him on Saturday. "He's the sharpest guy I've ever seen."

"Oh? In what way?"

"Well, to begin with, he's got a brilliant mind. He had his own business in California that was really successful. He's come up with several inventions that almost made him a fortune."

"In that case, how come he's so short of funds that he had to move in with you and your mother?" I demanded.

"Why, uh—he, uh, suffered some temporary setbacks. You know my uncle had a drinking problem, and apparently, while he was under the influence, he made a few major mistakes. Unfortunately, he sold the patent to his best invention before he knew how successful it was going to be. And then he got in with some bad characters who made some shady investments, and he wound up losing the business. He admits that none of this would have happened if he hadn't been drinking. That's why he came back to New York—to start all over and do it right, now that he's stopped drinking."

"Oh." I didn't know what to say to this. I had read books about people who lived the kind of life Lenny was describing, but I had never known anyone who really was that way. I didn't know what to make of it. If Lenny's uncle was really so brilliant, how could he have messed his life up so badly by drinking?

"And you should hear him talk!" Lenny continued. "He's so dynamic—and what a sense of humor! My mother told me that they once went away to a hotel together when they were younger. Art got to entertaining a few people with his funny stories, and pretty soon he had a whole crowd gathered around him. That night, the comedian the hotel had hired to entertain bombed out, and someone called for Art to come up and take his place. Art got up there on the stage like a professional and had everyone laughing hysterically. My mother said he was spectacular!"

"Then your mother's glad he's come to live with you?"

"No-oo. She put up a lot of opposition at first. Our apartment is small, and since there's only one bed in my bedroom, Art is sleeping out on one of the sofas in the living room. When Art's not drinking he eats a lot, and my mother's afraid he'll run out of money and expect us to feed him. She's also afraid that if he likes being with us he'll want to stay for a long time. But Art sweet-talked her and assured her he already has a job possibility working for someone in the same business he was in in California. He swore he'll find his own place the moment the job comes through. So my mother gave in, and there he is!''

"Wonderful. I suppose that means we can't even go up to your place anymore with him there."

"Of course not, silly." Lenny laughed and put his arm around me. "I told my uncle I had a girlfriend, and he even wants to meet you. How about we go over to my house and say hello?"

"Say hello? When?"

"Now. Uncle Art is busy fixing our TV set that's been broken. He'll be home all afternoon."

I agreed, but reluctantly. Something told me that Uncle Art was not a person I was going to be happy to know.

I felt very apprehensive as I waited for Lenny to open the door to his apartment. Not only was I going to have to face meeting his uncle, but his mother was going to be there as well.

Mrs. Lipoff and I didn't hit it off from the start. "So, this is your latest little girlfriend," she had said to Lenny when she first met me. She emphasized "latest" and "little" as if I were neither very important nor going to be around very long. She was so different from my mother that I didn't know what to make of her.

She looked sort of like Lenny, with the same smooth complexion, narrow nose, and large brown eyes. She was naturally pretty, but then she did all this horrible stuff she thought enhanced her looks: dying her hair silver, putting on tons of makeup, and painting her long nails in deep colors. I knew she had had a hard life and hadn't gotten along with Lenny's father. Now that they were separated, she was not getting along with Lenny. She had stopped cooking and doing his laundry last year after a big fight they had had. They both had terrible tempers and often wound up yelling and screaming at each other. When Mrs. Lipoff was angry at Lenny, she would also act as if she were angry at me. I never knew in what mood I was going to find her, so I tried to keep out of her way.

Today, however, she seemed in a decent mood as she greeted us at the door. "Oh, hello, dahr-ling. I haven't seen you in a while," she said to me.

I wanted to tell her it was better that way, but all I said was, "I probably wouldn't be here today either, but Lenny wanted me to meet his uncle."

"Oh, yes. Art's been working on fixing the TV all morning. He has such a wonderful mechanical mind, but he seems to have run into an impasse with our set. Come in, and I'll introduce you."

We went into the living room, which also served as Mrs. Lipoff's bedroom. A pile of linen on the extra sofa gave evidence to the fact that Uncle Art was now sleeping there as well.

Uncle Art looked up from where his head had

been buried in the back of the TV. He smiled charmingly when Lenny introduced us. "So this is the little girl I've heard so much about."

Maybe it was his choice of the word "little" to describe me, but Lenny's uncle reminded me very much of his mother. His features were similar to hers, as were his gestures, expressions, and the patronizing tone of his voice.

I was hoping Lenny would be content with a quick hello so we could escape quickly to his room, but no such luck. He sat down on one of the big chairs in the living room, and I had no choice but to sit on the other. I perched there uncomfortably while Mrs. Lipoff sat on a sofa plucking her eyebrows and admiring her reflection in a magnifying mirror. Uncle Art kept tinkering with the TV, muttering how the old-fashioned kind were so much easier to fix.

"I give up." He finally stood up and admitted defeat. "We've got to call in a TV repairman."

"I can't do that, Art," said Mrs. Lipoff. "Those guys charge an arm and a leg to begin with, and they always try to cheat you by saying you need something additional. I've dealt with TV repairmen before."

"Not with me around, you haven't." Art gave me a wink when he said this. "I know how to handle them—just leave it to me."

"I'm glad you said that, because I don't have any time to hang around here anymore." Mrs. Lipoff applied a liberal dusting of blusher, touched up her lipstick, and gave a last glance in the mirror. "I've got an appointment to keep."

"You've always got an appointment to keep," he scoffed. "So just get going while I get someone in here." Art got a number out of the Yellow Pages and made the call. Sounding as if he were someone very important, he managed to arrange to have a repairman come right to the house.

"This better not cost too much, Art," Mrs. Lipoff warned him as she piled a load of bracelets on each arm.

"I told you not to worry about it."

"Bye kids. Don't let Art chew your ears off!" She threw on her coat and breezed out the door.

Lenny and I were left with his uncle in the living room. Art didn't bother asking questions like how did I like school or what did I want to be when I grew up, the way most grown-ups would. Instead, he started telling us stories about himself: how he started a fast food business as soon as he got out of school; how he almost made a fortune at least five or six separate times, but something or someone always came along to ruin it.

I looked at Lenny and saw he was watching his uncle with a fascination that was almost worshipful. How could Lenny be impressed by someone who was so obviously a phony?

As I was thinking about this, the doorbell rang. "That must be the TV repairman," Art interrupted his own monologue. "Now you kids don't say a word. Leave everything to me."

"Hello. Speedy TV Repair, at your service." The repairman smiled pleasantly as Uncle Art ushered him into the living room.

"I'm Arthur Ames," he introduced himself.

"This TV is my sister's, but I told her I'd take care of having it fixed. I'm visiting here temporarily. I travel around the country for the Better Business Bureau."

"The BBB?" The repairman looked startled. "What do you do for them?"

"Oh, I supervise operations in the various of-fices. I review files and make sure they're accurate, check on complaints about specific businesses and see if they're valid—that sort of thing. The BBB is a pretty powerful organization, you know. We can make or break a business with our reports."

"I know." The repairman squirmed nervously. "Well, it's been nice talking to you. Let's see if I can find what's wrong with the TV."

He went to work under Art's watchful eye. "Here's the source of the trouble!" he announced after a short time. "Just a minor repair. It won't be expensive at all."

"That's good." Uncle Art beamed. "It's a plea-sure to do business with such an honest company!" He winked at Lenny and me as he paid the repair-man and ushered him to the door.

"How do you like the way I handled that sucker?" he asked when he returned. "It's one of my favorite methods of dealing with repairmen: Once they think you're affiliated with the BBB, they never cheat you. If anything, they under-charge!" He tipped his head back and laughed as if he was very pleased with himself.

"That was great, uncle!" Now Lenny looked really impressed. "I'll have to remember that one for when I get older!"

"Oh, I've got a lot of tricks to teach you while I'm here, my boy." Art playfully punched Lenny in the shoulder.

Watching the two of them, I felt more uncomfortable than ever. I had a sick feeling that despite Lenny's obvious delight at having his uncle around, his influence would bring nothing but trouble.

Chapter

Nine

It didn't take long for Lenny's uncle to start creating the problems I had feared. About a week after Uncle Art's arrival, Lenny stopped telling everyone what a sharp, brilliant, and wonderful guy he was. A week after that, Lenny mentioned that as bad as it was living with his mother, having both his mother and his uncle there was much worse. Soon after that, he was telling nothing but horror stories about how awful it was living with his uncle, who had started to drink again.

"I figured something was wrong when his behavior kept getting more and more bizarre," he confessed to me and Sheldon one night as we were walking together to pick up Roz for a double date. This was something we did less frequently now that Sheldon had moved away. Whether it was the distance or Roz's increasing involvement with her school, Fine Arts, that caused this situation, I didn't know. But the two of them definitely seemed to be drifting apart.

"Like what?" asked Sheldon. Surprisingly, his friendship with Lenny and the other boys didn't seem adversely affected by his move. He would spend whole weekends with them, hanging around the poolroom that was open all night, or sleeping over at one of their apartments, so he got to see them almost as much as he had before. He was particularly close to Lenny and concerned about what went on in his home.

"Like starting to scream and pick on me or my mother with no provocation. Like nodding off to sleep in the middle of the afternoon. Like having blackouts—not remembering what he said or did. Like doing crazy things like painting the kitchen without covering anything up and winding up ruining pots, dishes, and appliances. Like having uncontrollable tantrums, throwing things, breaking things, and even cutting up my mother's clothes."

"Wow. That does sound crazy," I said. "But how do you know it's because he's drinking again?"

"I thought I smelled alcohol on him a few times, but I wasn't sure. Then today, the toilet wasn't working right so I opened the tank to see if I could fix it. Inside, I found two bottles of vodka, one half-full and one completely empty. It's obvious he's been hiding the liquor there and drinking it while pretending to go to the bathroom. That explains his crazy behavior. He's drunk all the time."

"Did you say anything to anyone about it?" asked Sheldon.

"Not yet. I don't think it's going to do any good to talk to my uncle. He'll only find another hiding place for his liquor if he wants to drink. I'm not sure if I should say anything to my mother, either."

"Maybe if you do she'll kick him out and your problems with him will be over," I suggested.

"I don't think she's strong enough to do that," he answered. "She demanded he get out at least a hundred times the past month, and he just laughs. She's not strong enough to do anything but fight with him. It's pure torture living in my house. It's a good thing report cards came out already so I was able to keep my grades high enough to stay on the bowling team. With the way things have been going at home, it's impossible to concentrate on anything to do with school."

"Lenny! That report card was only the midterm grade. The final grades are the ones that count! If you allow yourself to slip now, you'll ruin everything you've worked for. You've got to get things straightened out at home!" I said anxiously.

"You're probably right," he said grimly. "But telling my mother's not the answer. She'd only—"

"Hey, can we change the subject now?" Sheldon interrupted as we arrived at Roz's building. "Roz and I haven't been getting along well recently. I want this evening to get us back on the right track again. Let's try to talk about pleasant things."

"Sure, Sheldon," we agreed. I felt as if I had a vested interest in keeping Roz and Sheldon together. Joel and Penny had broken up two weeks ago, and Joel was back to his usual routine of playing the field. Billy and Donna weren't getting along. Roz and Sheldon were the last "couple friends" we had left. If they broke up Lenny would be the only one of his close friends to have a steady girlfriend. I knew the kind of pressure the boys were capable of putting on him if they felt he was spending too much time with me and not enough with them. That was not the type of thing that was beneficial to our relationship.

It had been a few weeks since I had last seen Roz, and you could tell from the moment she appeared at the door that she had changed. For one thing, she dressed strangely. Instead of wearing jeans, a shirt, and sneakers, the way the rest of us did, she was dressed in an "artsy" style, typical of where she went to school. She had on a black turtleneck sweater, heavy silver jewelry, a long, printed skirt, and black shoes that could only be described as "weird."

"Hi, Roz! You look, uh, different!" was all I could say.

"Like it?" Roz twirled around so we could appreciate her new look from every angle.

"I don't," Sheldon said bluntly. "You look like some sort of freak. If you walk out like that everyone's going to be staring at you. I want you to change right now."

At one time this approach might have worked with Roz. Now, however, she had too much of a sense of her own independence to be intimidated by Sheldon.

"I will not! I'm entitled to dress any way I want to, Sheldon—and this is the way I choose to dress.

Just remember which one of us is the artistic one in our relationship, which one of us has the sense of style! I'll have you know the boys at school, who have an appreciation of the finer things in life, know what style is!''

"Oh they know what style is, do they?'' Sheldon went mincing around the room, waving his hands. "Well, you don't say? Tell me, sweetheart, if those boys are so artistic and cultured and all that, why aren't you going out with them tonight instead of with poor, unsophisticated me?'' He glared at her.

She glared right back. "I certainly don't know. I guess I thought I'd see if we could rekindle something between us for old times' sake. But now I can see I was utterly mistaken!''

I could feel the tension building between them. It was obvious that if something wasn't done immediately, the entire evening would be ruined. I glanced at Lenny, hoping for some assistance from him, but he was too busy laughing at the sight of Sheldon and Roz bristling at one another to be of help.

"Hey, guys. Cut it out.'' I stepped between them. "It's silly to fight over something as insignificant as clothes. Look, Sheldon, Roz has a point. She's entitled to dress any way she wants, and you shouldn't demand that she change. But Roz, you've got to understand that Sheldon's not used to seeing you dress this way, and it might take him a while to come to appreciate it. So why doesn't everyone take it easy and give the other person a chance? I bet at the end of the evening, you won't even think about what Roz is wearing, Sheldon. Maybe you'll even come to like it!''

"Like it? Never!" Sheldon growled. But he did agree to let Roz wear whatever she wanted and to take her out as planned.

Despite Sheldon's promise to give Roz's "new look" a chance, he took a position next to Lenny and away from her as we walked to the movie theater. Roz walked next to me.

"Why did you have to dress this way tonight, Roz?" I couldn't help asking her while Lenny and Sheldon were busy discussing some boring details about Sunday's upcoming football game. "You might have known it would upset Sheldon."

"And why should I have to worry about whether or not it upsets Sheldon?" she demanded. "I'm my own person. I like artsy things and that includes artsy clothing. I have a right to wear what I want. I don't have to always dress in a jeans uniform the way the rest of you do!"

I felt as if this were almost a personal attack. "Roz! I don't wear jeans because it's a uniform. I love jeans—I always have since I was a little kid. They're comfortable; you never have to worry about what goes with them or about getting them dirty. I wear jeans because I want to!"

"Maybe you do." Roz shrugged. "But I still refuse to look like everyone else. Either Sheldon can accept that or he can't. I'm not going to change for him or anyone else."

I guess I could have argued that, in a sense, Roz's way of dressing was a uniform for "artsy" types as well. It didn't seem worth it, however. It certainly wasn't going to contribute anything toward having this evening turn out the way I wanted it to. So I changed the subject by asking her a question about her art history class.

Once we were in the theater, things seemed to get back to normal. Maybe because it was too dark in there for Sheldon to focus on Roz's clothes. Or maybe it was because everyone gets along better when they're making out. At any rate, it wasn't long before I noticed that Sheldon and Roz were into some hot and heavy kissing. After that I was too busy with Lenny to worry about them.

There's something about the movies that makes me feel romantic, especially when the picture is a love story like the one we were watching that night. I looked at Lenny's face, bathed in the soft, flickering light reflected from the screen, and I was filled with love for him.

It was almost four months now since Lenny and I had gone back together, the longest period for us without a major fight or breakup. Despite the problems Lenny was having at home, we had been getting along so well that I could hardly believe it. I was so glad we weren't completely removed from one another like Danny and Fran, or constantly fighting like Billy and Donna, or having philosophical differences like Sheldon and Roz. Despite the fact that Lenny and I were opposites in many ways, when things were good we complemented each other well. I was so happy to have him for my boyfriend.

By the time the movie ended, Roz and Sheldon were obviously feeling good about each other, too, because they left the theater holding hands and smiling. I guess even Lenny wanted to prolong the evening, because instead of taking us home quickly, so he and Sheldon could rush to the poolroom and meet the rest of the boys, he suggested that we all go get something to eat.

We went to Nick's Coffee Shop, the place that served the best ice cream in the neighborhood. I especially liked Nick's because you could sit at tables upstairs on a cute little balcony.

We got my favorite table, right by the balcony railing. It was fun to look down and watch the people coming in and out as we ate our ice cream. Lenny was in high spirits and kept up a running commentary on everyone, predicting what they were going to buy.

"See that fat one—she's not going to be content with just a cone. I bet it's a double banana split for her and a half-gallon of chocolate chocolate chip to take home. And see that skinny one—she'll just get a single scoop of plain vanilla, but she'll splurge on a sugar cone!" We all rolled with laughter when his predictions came out reversed. The fat one bought a cone, and the skinny one sat down with a huge banana split.

"Well, at least I was right about one thing," Lenny reminded us. "The fat one picked chocolate chocolate chip as her flavor!" Somehow, this struck us as funny, and we all began laughing agian.

"Oh, and look at those two weird-looking guys," Lenny interrupted our laughter to point out. "They won't be satisfied with any ordinary flavor. I bet it's rum raisin or Mandarin orange, or maybe tutti-frutti for them!"

This remark started a whole new round of laughter. The two guys were kind of weird-looking. One was dressed totally in black and the other in bright, flashy colors.

"Tutti-frutti! Ha-ha-ha!" Sheldon laughed so hard he almost fell from his seat.

It took me a while to realize that Roz was no longer laughing with us. Instead, she was staring at the two boys. "Why, I think that's—I know those guys!" she announced. She got up from her seat and hung over the balcony railing. "Peter! Julian!" she called.

Startled, the boys looked up. When they saw it was Roz, they both began to smile. The one in the colors was actually pretty cute. "Roz!" he exclaimed. "What are you doin' here?"

"I live in this neighborhood. What are you doing here?"

"Julian and I came to see a foreign film at the Town Art Cinema," he explained. "It's not far from here. You must go there often."

"Not really. It's hard to find people willing to go with me to see quality films." Roz glanced meaningfully at Sheldon, then turned her attention back to Peter. "How was the movie?"

"Great!" Peter exclaimed. "Say, if you like foreign movies, you can come with us some time. Julian and I try to see every major film that comes around, don't we, Julian?"

"But of course! Got to keep on top of the cultural scene," Julian agreed.

"Wonderful. I'll keep it in mind next time something's playing I really want to see." Roz smiled warmly at the two boys. "Hey, if you guys aren't doing anything right now, why don't you come up here and I'll introduce you to everyone?"

If Roz had been watching Sheldon's face, which had been turning all sorts of sickly shades of green while she had been talking to Peter, I don't think she would have made that suggestion. But apparently she was too engrossed in what was going on below to notice. She only became aware of Sheldon again when he rammed his elbow into her back.

"Ooof," she gasped, as she fell forward against the railing, which was fortunately high enough to keep her from flipping over. She whirled around angrily. "Hey! Why did you do that, Sheldon?"

"Sorry. It was an accident." His expression made it quite clear that it wasn't.

She glared at him as if she had a lot more to say, but turned her attention back to Peter and Julian. They seemed to realize there was something going on on the balcony they were better off not becoming a part of.

"No thanks, Roz. We've really got to get going now. We'll see you in school on Monday and discuss things further." The two of them took their ice cream cones, which were plain chocolate and vanilla, and left the store with a last wave to Roz.

Roz kept hanging on to the railing, even after they were gone. A strained silence settled over our table. You could feel the tension in the air.

"You were wrong again, Lenny. Those two got vanilla and chocolate, not tutti-frutti," I said, in an attempt to break the tension.

It didn't work. No one laughed this time. Roz

107

turned around and glared at Sheldon. "The nerve of you," she began. You could see she was struggling to control her temper. "Peter and Julian had to have seen you poking me when I invited them up here. It was completely obvious you didn't want them. How could you be so rude?"

Sheldon looked from Roz to Lenny and back to Roz again. "Oh, so you think I was rude to your little artsy boys, did you? Well, isn't that too bad! What the heck do you call it when you're supposed to be out on a date with me and you wind up hanging over a balcony playing Juliet to some freaked-up Romeo? And what do you mean saying you'll go to a movie with those two next time? No girl of mine is ever going to be seen with the likes of garbage like that!"

This was the wrong thing to say to newly-liberated Roz. I knew there was no way she would take Sheldon's threats, especially after having been sought after by the two Fine Arts boys.

"That statement exemplifies the trouble with our relationship, Sheldon. You think because we're going together you have the right to order me around. Well, I'm telling you now that what I'm getting out of this relationship is no longer worth the hassle. I've had it. We're through!" Having said this, she grabbed her pocketbook and raced down the steps and out the door.

Sheldon, Lenny, and I sat looking at each other, completely stunned. Just moments ago, we had all been laughing together, having a good time. And now everything was ruined by a stupid misunderstanding.

"Sheldon, go after her," I begged. "Tell her you didn't mean to order her around. Make things right again, before they go too far."

"They've gone too far already," he said grimly. "I've seen this coming for a long time. Roz has really gotten into that whole art scene at school this year and resents me because I'm not like the cultured freaks she associates with there. She's changed so much that it had to affect our relationship. I don't think it'll ever work for us again."

"But Sheldon, it has to!" I said desperately. "I mean, you love each other, don't you? You've been going together too long to throw it all away. You've got to get back together—you've got to!"

I looked at Sheldon, but his face was completely hardened. Whatever love he had had for Roz had been replaced by something else. I knew this was it for them, and it worried me.

Sheldon was the friend who was closest to Lenny. The fact that he was no longer going with Roz couldn't possibly be beneficial to my relationship with Lenny.

Chapter

Ten

Although I felt a void in my life at not having Roz and Sheldon as a couple anymore, December brought some consolations. It was Christmas vacation, and all the kids who had gone away to college would be coming home again. Social activities would be picking up.

Danny showed up at my doorstep early Saturday morning the first weekend he was back from school. "Danny!" I shrieked, rushing into his arms for a hug.

Then I stood back and looked him over. He was still way too chubby, but he actually looked pretty good to me—older, more sophisticated and worldly.

I took him into the kitchen to say hello to my parents, who were still eating breakfast. They looked even happier to see him than I was.

"Sit down, Danny. Let me get you something to

eat.'' My mother pushed a plate of rolls, muffins, and bagels in front of him. ''Tell us all about college—it must be so exciting!''

Danny dug right in, spreading a heavy layer of cream cheese on a blueberry muffin, polishing it off, and then reaching for a bagel. He felt right at home with my parents. What a difference from the atmosphere when Lenny was in my house. My parents loved Danny.

''Exciting? Well, I guess you could say that,'' he managed to reply between bites. ''You're exposed to so many brilliant minds, so many challenging theories. But it's hard work. I find I have to devote almost all my attention to schoolwork and I have hardly any time for social activities. That's why I was really looking forward to coming home and cutting loose again with all my favorite girls!''

He looked at me suggestively when he said that and reached out to grab my hand. His grasp felt wet and greasy, and I pulled away fast. ''Ugh! What have you got on your hand, Danny?''

He looked. ''Oh, it's only some cream cheese. Here, I'll let you lick it off for me.'' He stuck his hand in front of my face.

I pulled back disgustedly. ''Yuck, Danny. Do you have to be so gross so soon after your arrival?'' I grabbed a napkin and wiped my hand.

Danny laughed and licked off his own fingers. Surprisingly, my parents, who are normally sticklers for proper table manners, didn't seem disturbed by his actions. If only they could be so tolerant of Lenny!

''Perhaps now that you're home, you and Linda

could go out together," my mother suggested. "She's spending entirely too much time with—with that boy."

"His name is Lenny, Ma," I told her, for what must have been the millionth time. I felt like kicking my mother under the table. I didn't need her to put ideas into Danny's head about a possible romantic involvement with me.

As I feared, Danny picked right up on her idea. "That's just why I came over here! I was hoping you'd come to the theater with me tonight, Linda. We could stand on the line in Times Square and get discount tickets to a play." Danny smiled at me, revealing that he had not yet swallowed the mass of chewed-up bagel and cream cheese. It really turned me off.

"I can't, Danny. Tonight Chris Berland is giving a party for the kids in the neighborhood at his house." I was grateful to have this excuse handy. "But you can come—the main purpose is to get everyone together now that all you guys are back from college."

"Will Fran be there?" Danny perked up immediately. Apparently, he was still interested in her although their entire relationship had been reduced to the exchange of an occasional letter.

"I think so. She said she was going when we spoke about it last. But don't be disappointed if she's nothing like you expect her to be, Danny. Fran has done a lot of changing since you last saw her."

"Probably everyone has, except for you, Linda." My mother shook her head as she started to clear the table. I guess even she was sick of watching Danny eat. "Would you believe she's still in love with that boy, Danny? I keep hoping someday she'll wake up and see him for what he is!"

"Ma, come on! Let's not start this again," I said, exasperated. If you asked me, it was my parents who couldn't see things the way they were. They were willing to overlook all Danny's faults because they liked him and he did well in school. They were willing to overlook nothing about Lenny.

I didn't let my negative feelings about my parents put a damper on my good mood as I got ready to go to the party. It was going to be so great to have everyone together again. Our crowd hadn't had a party for a long time. With the coming of the cold weather, most of the kids didn't hang out as much anymore. Everyone was busy with homework, after-school activities, and studying for exams. We needed this party to get things going again.

The party started out just fine. Everyone from our original crowd showed up, including Donna, Roz, and Fran. Fran took the pressure off me by being very open with Danny: sitting on his lap, eating off his plate, and flirting with him shamelessly. Danny looked as if he was really enjoying it, but I was worried that he would get his hopes up too high and wind up getting hurt. I knew Fran was having too much of a good time dating different boys to want to attach herself to Danny again.

Faring less well than Danny and Fran were Roz and Sheldon. This was the first time they had been in the same room together since that scene in Nick's. They might as well have been at different ends of the world. They kept so far apart you wouldn't even know they were acquainted unless you noticed they were watching each other carefully out of the corners of their eyes, making sure they kept out of each other's way.

Donna and Billy were getting along for a change; so, except for the undercurrent between Roz and Sheldon, there was no tension in the room. Everyone was filling each other in on what had been going on since the last time we'd all been together. Everyone was dancing and having a great time.

I danced with Lenny and with the other boys, too. I was too busy enjoying myself to notice that he and some of the other boys kept watching the door with an air of expectation.

I was unaware that anything unusual had been planned for this party until I saw a bunch of boys rushing to the door. Everyone began to follow them to see what was going on.

Joel Fudd and Geno Sharp, one of the boys who had come home from college, had made their grand entrance. It wasn't they who were creating the commotion, however; it was what they had brought with them. They were each carrying an armload of six-packs of beer!

When I saw this, it was as if a red flag of warning popped up in my head. Beer—alcohol—trouble! The associations were immediate, and they were strong. We had never had alcohol at our parties before, and we had all managed to have a good time. As far as I was concerned, those guys were asking for nothing but trouble by bringing around all that beer.

I guess most of the other kids didn't share my opinion because they all gathered around Geno, who seemed to be in charge. "This is what we do in college to inject life into our parties," he announced, holding up a can of beer. Everyone cheered and pushed forward to get some.

I wasn't surprised by the fact that most of the boys wanted to drink; they were always doing stuff they thought made them look "macho." What surprised me was seeing so many of the girls join in, too. I was glad to see that Roz and Donna kept far away from the beer, but Fran was one of the first to go up and get one.

I got her aside in one corner of Chris's living room. "Fran, why are you drinking that beer, anyway?"

"Because it's here," she laughed. "And I like it!"

"Like it? You mean you like the way it tastes?" My nose wrinkled in disgust at the smell of the stuff.

"Well, not exactly—although it really isn't that bad once you get into it. But it's like Geno said— beer drinking's what the kids do at college when they want to have a good time. I've been dating a few college boys recently, so I had to get used to it. If I didn't, they'd look at me as if I were some kind of unsophisticated little kid."

She took a sip from the can as she said this, and I could tell by the way she inadvertently screwed up her face that she didn't really like it. Fran might think that drinking made her look older and more sophisticated, but she was wrong. Fran was even shorter than I was, and she looked younger than her age. The can of beer in her hand made her look silly—like a little girl dressed up in her mother's clothing and stumbling around in high heels.

I saw I was getting nowhere with Fran, so I turned around to look for Lenny. I found him on the line waiting to get a beer.

"Lenny!" I rushed right over and grabbed him by the arm. "May I talk to you for a moment, in private, right now?"

Lenny looked over at the beer supply as if to assure himself there was enough left so he could still get one before he stepped off the line. "Okay, okay. What is it that's so urgent?"

I led him to the corner where I had been previously talking to Fran. "It's the beer, Lenny. I didn't know there was going to be any at this party."

"Is that all that's bothering you?" he laughed. "Come on, Linda. You know how it is when these guys go off to college. They're so used to drinking that they don't think a party's a party unless the alcohol is flowing. But don't worry about it, you don't have to drink if you don't want to."

"I don't. But I don't want you to drink either."

"Oh no? Well, why the heck not?"

It was immediately obvious that Lenny found my request threatening. I knew I had to be very careful. The last thing I wanted was for him to feel I was trying to boss him around by telling him not to drink. That could very well make him drink even more.

"It's not that I want to tell you what to do, Lenny," I explained quickly. "It's only that this is

116

the first time we've had alcohol at our parties, and it's kind of scary to me. I'm sure in the future it'll be easier for me to deal with—if we make it through this party without any disasters. Plea-ease, Lenny, just this once.''

I guess this was the right approach to take. Even though Lenny thought my fears were silly, he was willing to go along with my request—just this once. As the night wore on, I was thankful he had the opportunity to view this party with a clear head so he could really see the effect alcohol was having on our friends.

The jokes they were laughing so hard at were not really funny, but silly and stupid, and the behaviors they were laughing at were, too. But silly and stupid were one thing—it was easy to laugh at that kind of stuff. The problem occurred when the alcohol helped turn silly and stupid to mean, boisterous, and cruel.

The first incident came when a slightly drunk Sheldon stopped avoiding Roz and began following her around, taunting her unmercifully. ''Who told you to show your ugly face here at this party, Miss Fancy Buttons? We don't want anyone tainted by association with weirdo artsy-boys hanging around with us.''

Roz kept trying to get out of Sheldon's way, but he wouldn't let her. He kept coming after her for more.

''Come on, Sheldon, leave Roz alone. She hasn't done anything to you,'' Lenny said, trying to calm Sheldon down. But Sheldon was beyond calming. The alcohol had distorted his normally easygoing personality. He was like a man consumed by a mission—a mission to make life miserable for Roz.

It didn't take too much of this before Roz decided she'd had enough. "I knew it was a mistake to expect you to act civil," she said to Sheldon as she picked up her coat from a pile that was tossed over a chair. "I hope you're satisfied. I'm leaving because of you, and it'll be a long time before you see me around here again!"

"Suits me fine!" Sheldon laughed viciously. "I don't want to see you here or anyplace else I have to go, for that matter. Get lost and stay lost!"

Roz threw on her coat and was about to start for the door when Donna came running after her. "Wait, Roz! I'll go with you! I've had about all I can take from this maniac for tonight!"

The "maniac" she was referring to was Billy, who was following closely at her heels. I had been so engrossed with Sheldon and Roz, I hadn't noticed that a fight had started between Billy and Donna as well. It must have been going on for a while, because they were both red-faced and furious when they reached the door.

"Just where do you think you're going?" Billy demanded. Donna's reply was to extract her coat, which was a new one I hadn't seen before, from the pile, and start putting it on.

This infuriated Billy even more. "Oh, no you don't!" he shouted, grabbing the coat by one sleeve.

"Give me my coat!" Donna tried to pull it away from him. His grip was too strong. He tugged and she tugged. The next thing we heard was a ripping sound as the stitching gave way and the entire sleeve tore off at the shoulder.

Donna looked from the coat, which she held in her hand, to the sleeve, which Billy held in his, with horror. "My new coat! It was a Christmas present from my parents! They'll absolutely kill me!" she moaned.

Billy seemed sobered by what he had done. He handed the sleeve back to Donna. "It can probably be fixed," was the closest he came to apologizing. Then he added, "But you deserved it, anyway."

Donna then did a brave but crazy thing: She grabbed the coat sleeve from Billy, then reached out and slapped him across the face with it—hard enough so the sound could be heard across the room. Then she and Roz left, slamming the door behind them.

Billy was so stunned that he stood there rubbing his face and staring at the door. Then he became aware that everyone was looking at him. "She's not going to get away with that!" he yelled. "Wait till I—" He began sifting through the pile of coats, tossing them all over the floor as he attempted to locate his.

Fortunately, Chris was close enough to step in and stop Billy. Chris was a big, strong guy, but he could also be gentle, and he knew how to respect girls. "Hey, cool it." He put a restraining hand on Billy's shoulder.

"Get away from me, man!" Billy whirled around furiously, ready to strike out. But he calmed down when he saw it was Chris, probably the only person in the room he would have trouble beating in a fight. "I can't find my coat."

"It's probably not there. I took a bunch of coats into my bedroom," Chris explained. "But why would you want to run after Donna now, anyway? Let her go home. She feels bad enough that you ripped her coat. You're better off staying here, where you can have a good time."

This idea seemed to appeal to Billy. "Yeah, you're right. Let her freeze out there in the street. I don't need the likes of her to have fun. Just hand me another beer!"

I wanted to tell him that it was probably the beer that helped cause all the trouble in the first place, but I thought better of it. I didn't need Billy to turn his anger on me.

The party ended without any further disasters. But the fun had gone out of it. I wondered if anyone else felt as I did: It had been so much better before the boys brought the beer.

New Year's Eve was approaching, and no one had come forward to volunteer their house for a party. Perhaps it was because of the bad taste left by the events at Chris's party, or perhaps it was that most parents, like mine, were going to be home and didn't want a bunch of teenagers up at their house. At any rate, it was two days before New Year's, and no one had plans to do anything.

New Year's Eve was especially important to me this year because Lenny and I had had such a bad one the year before. Then, too, there had been no plans until the last minute, so I had accepted a babysitting job. At the last minute, when Jessie had decided to have a party, I could only get away for a few hours. Those hours were anything but romantic. I had gotten jealous because Lenny was flirting with an old girlfriend, and we had had a big fight and almost broken up over it. I didn't want this New Year's to be anything like that one.

Lenny didn't either. Instead of counting on the crowd's coming up with something, he asked me if I wanted to go out, just the two of us. "We'll have dinner in a Chinese restaurant, take a walk up Fifth Avenue to see all the store windows decorated for Christmas, and then go to Times Square to see the apple come down for the New Year. It'll be fun!"

It did sound like fun to me—and romantic. It was a miracle to me that Lenny would come up with such a wonderful idea on his own. It was this kind of thing I had always yearned for in our relationship. Finally, Lenny seemed to be turning into the kind of loving, compassionate boyfriend I had always wanted him to be.

I was so happy with our plans that even when, the day before New Year's, Joel Fudd decided we could have a party up at his house after all, I didn't want to go. Joel's parents weren't going to be home and Joel liked to drink—I had enough of the problems that combination could lead to. Besides, none of my best friends, Roz, Fran, and Donna, were going to be there. Roz and Donna didn't want to go anywhere Sheldon and Billy would be, and Fran had a date with a college boy she had met. "Let's just stick to our original plans," I said to Lenny. "We'll have a better time by ourselves."

I was right to choose to spend New Year's this way, I couldn't help thinking as I walked up Fifth Avenue hand in hand with Lenny. It was a cold night, and a soft snow began falling from the dark winter sky. The snow, coupled with the gaily-colored lights lining the streets and the carols playing in the air, made the night seem almost magical. It was easy to get lost in the fairyland scenes that filled the windows of the big department stores. Animated figures, dressed in costumes of Christmases long past, shopped for presents, skated on a frozen lake, danced at a party, decorated a Christmas tree, and climbed into bed to await the arrival of Santa Claus.

Lenny and I stood there, noses pressed against the glass windows, taking in every detail. "Oh, look at that little dog there, wagging his tail," I pointed out, not wanting Lenny to miss a thing.

"And look at the children peeking over the railing, watching the grownups dance," he said to me.

We laughed together at the fat Santa, trying to get down the chimney, and at all the other funny scenes. I don't think I had ever had a better time with Lenny. He put his arm around me as we walked, and I didn't even mind how cold I was or the fact that my feet were getting soaked from the accumulating snow. But Lenny noticed I was shivering and steered me to a restaurant so we could both warm up.

We sat there, drinking hot chocolate and gazing

into one another's eyes. We probably would have stayed there right through New Year's if the manager didn't come over to tell us he was closing for the night.

"I can't believe it, it's almost eleven-thirty!" Lenny said when he saw the time. "We're going to have to hurry if we want to get to Times Square before midnight."

We were lucky enough to find a taxi to take us to the Times Square area, and we raced the last couple of blocks on foot. The crowd awaiting the traditional signaling of the new year was too big for us to get up close, but by weaving under arms and around barricades, Lenny got us to where we could have a good view. You could feel the excitement building as midnight grew near, and there were so many people packing the street that I no longer felt the cold.

Finally, the big moment arrived. Everyone counted backward from ten as the ball descended, exploded, and flashed the new year. "Happy New Year!" people kept yelling, while blowing on noise-makers and horns.

"Happy New Year," I whispered to Lenny. He kissed me, and I forgot about the noise and the crowds around us. I only knew it was wonderful to be with the boy I loved, this day and every day of the year.

It wasn't until later, when we were riding home on the subway, that I gave any thought at all as to what my friends might be doing. This was the first

New Year's I had spent without them since we had become a group.

That thought made me feel a little sad, but I pushed it from my mind. I was together with Lenny, and we had had a perfect New Year's. That was what really mattered.

Chapter

Eleven

After New Year's came my least favorite time of the year. With the removal of the seasonal decorations, lights, and music, there were only the days of bleak, cold, gray winter to look forward to. Our crowd's activities dwindled down even further as the weather grew too miserable to stay out for long, the college boys returned to school, and we who were left got busy studying for exams.

Exam time always brought tension to my relationship with Lenny. Because school was so important to me, I really wanted him to do what I thought was best for him—start achieving the good grades he was capable of getting. I had learned that it was useless to nag him about studying: he would only get mad at me, we would wind up having a fight, and it wouldn't make him study anyway. But I still couldn't let go of the issue completely. I tried to find more subtle ways to trick him into studying.

"I've got this big exam coming up at the end of the week, Lenny. I've got to study for it, but I also want to be with you. If you come up to my house and study with me, I'll make it worth your while."

There were two ways I had found to make studying worth Lenny's while. One was to find some snack to feed him, which wasn't too difficult since my mother kept the kitchen well stocked. The other was to get my brothers out of their room so we could do some making out while we were studying. Fortunately, to some extent, my mother cooperated in setting this up. She was so glad we were doing our schoolwork that she insisted my brothers stay out of the room and leave us in peace.

Of course, she also insisted that the door to the room remain open and that we sit on chairs while studying instead of on the much more comfortable beds. Still, we managed to steal some wonderful kisses together while keeping our ears tuned in to the sound of the loose wooden boards in the hallway that warned us if someone was approaching. At the first squeak, we would pull apart and look as if we were deeply engrossed in our work.

Despite these less than desirable studying conditions, I was able to keep my average above 90, as was usual for me. The day that report cards were given out, Ms. Morgan, my homeroom teacher, asked me to stay and talk to her after the other kids had left. I was a little nervous waiting to hear what she had to say until her smile assured me it wasn't going to be anything bad.

"I noticed something very interesting while going over your report card, Linda. You're a year ahead of yourself in most of your major subjects."

"That's because the school I went to before Tech had an advanced curriculum," I explained.

"Well, whatever the reason, the point I want to make is this: With the exception of English, you'll have finished all of your high school requirements at the end of your junior year. Of course, we do offer enough college level courses here at Tech so that you could fill a program for your senior year, regardless. But the way I see it, all you have to do is double up in English—taking both eleventh and twelfth grade English together each term—and you should be able to graduate at the end of next year and go right on to college."

"Really?" This was an idea that had tremendous appeal to me. Graduating a year earlier would bring me one year closer to the time I could realistically consider getting married to Lenny. "That would be wonderful! How do I go about arranging to double up in English?"

"Well, I'm not even sure if they'd allow it here at Tech; I've never heard of its being done. But your case should be an exception. It would be a shame to hold you back for one class. Why don't you go talk to your guidance counselor, Mrs. Eliot, and see what she suggests."

As soon as I thanked Ms. Morgan for bringing the matter to my attention, I went straight to Mrs. Eliot's office.

"Yes, I see what Ms. Morgan told you is valid," Mrs. Eliot said, gazing at me over her bifocals, after studying my records. "But we have a policy here at Tech of no acceleration. Instead, we pride ourselves on the large number of college-level courses we offer. You could acquire a number of credits right here. Most colleges would recognize them, although you might have to take a proficiency exam to prove you knew the material."

"Why should I do that?" I asked. "It makes more sense to graduate early and go right on to college. Then I don't have to worry about what credits they'll accept or taking extra exams."

"It might make sense, but as I told you, it's against Tech policy to allow early graduation. We can't afford to start a precedent—if you accelerate, other bright students will want to as well. If graduating early is that important to you, I'm afraid you'll have to transfer to your neighborhood high school. They don't have our high standards and will probably allow you to graduate with minimal requirements."

"My neighborhood high school?" That was Washington, the school where Lenny went. Even if he passed everything now, he was already so far behind it would take him an extra year to graduate, which meant we could go to school together next year. It would be the way I had always fantasized: Lenny and I riding on the bus together, having lunch together, maybe even having some classes together. I didn't think I could get my parents to accept the idea too readily, but what if I could?

Lenny and I, going to school together. It would be wonderful!

I had spent so much time in Mrs. Eliot's office

that I arrived home much later than I expected to. I found Lenny waiting where we had arranged to meet in the back of the candy store. Billy was with him, and he was not in a good mood. Lenny started right in by getting on me for being late.

"Didn't you tell me you were going to meet me here before three? Well, it's after four now. Where were you? Partying with some of those creepy Tech boys?"

"Of course not!" I was hurt that Lenny thought this of me. "Something unexpected came up about my program, and I had to check with my guidance counselor. I'm sorry to be late, but it was really important!"

"Oh? And what was so important that it was worth blowing an afternoon alone together I had planned? My uncle was out today, which would have given us a rare opportunity to be together at my house—that is, if you had shown up on time!"

"Oh, Lenny. I'm sorry. I didn't know your uncle was going to be out." The opportunities Lenny and I had to be alone together these days were so few that we tried to take advantage of every one of them. "But listen to this: My teacher pointed out to me that I'm ahead in every subject but English. If they would let me double up in English next year, I could graduate a year early. Wouldn't that be great?"

"I guess," Lenny said in a tone that made me feel he didn't think it was so great at all. I realized that this might be just one more example to him of how much better I did in school than he did, a situation he often found threatening. And maybe that was another thing that was putting him in a bad mood. He should have gotten his report card today, too. What if he had gotten another lousy one? ''So, are you?''

''Am I what?'' I had lost my train of thought.

''Graduating a year earlier. Will they let you?''

''Not if I stay at Tech. They have some ridiculously inflexible policy against it. But I could if I transfer to Washington.''

''Washington? You mean my Washington?''

''Of course. What do you think, Lenny? It looks as if you'll be in Washington another year. We could have such fun going there together.''

His obvious lack of enthusiasm increased my fears about his grades. ''I don't know. It could create some problems, too.''

''Problems? Like what?''

''Like being around each other too much. Like getting in each other's way and causing fights.''

''Like what happened with Donna and me,'' Billy chimed in. ''She was always watching me, checking to see if I was going to class, doing my work. I couldn't breathe with her around. That's why we broke up.''

''Oh, is *that* why you broke up, Billy?'' I replied. ''Somehow, I thought it was because you were mean to her and did violent things like ripping her coat. I guess I was mistaken.''

Billy didn't like this remark at all. ''Once again, Lipoff, your girlfriend is opening her big mouth. You'd better learn to control her before she gets to Washington, or I'll guarantee you nothing but trouble. Good luck. You're going to need it to deal with

130

her!" He took a last gulp from his soda, then put the bottle down and left the store.

"Why did you have to talk that way to Billy?" asked Lenny, obviously further irritated by what had just taken place. "He's my friend whether you like him or not."

"It's not that I don't like him," I tried to explain. "It's that I don't like the way he treats girls. And don't think it doesn't rub off on you, either. He stirs you up against me. Take that remark about your needing good luck to deal with me. What did he mean by that?"

Lenny busied himself dunking some french fries into a huge mound of ketchup he had dumped on his plate. The tension was thick between us. "Billy was referring to report cards," he said finally. "He only has to worry about showing his to his parents. I've got to worry about my mother's reactions, and I've also got to worry about your reaction!"

I got a sick, sinking feeling in my stomach as I realized where this conversation was leading. I took a deep breath. "You don't have to worry about me, Lenny—it's your report card, not mine. Why don't you just tell me how bad it is so we can get this over with real fast?"

But Lenny wasn't the type to get things over with fast. He made a big production out of sliding his report card out of his pocket and putting it, face-down, on the table. I reached for it, but he covered it with his hand. "Promise me you won't get mad at me."

"Lenny! Stop it! It's this game-playing that's getting me mad. Just show me the darn thing!"

He removed his hand and let me pick up the report card. It was even worse than I had feared. Out of all his subjects, he had only passed history and English. He had failed everything else, including gym!

I was stunned. I hadn't expected this. "Lenny! What happened? You had a 'C' average at midterm. How could you have gone downhill so fast?"

"It was easy. Midterm grades came out before things really got bad at home. With my uncle there and creating constant scenes, it became impossible for me to keep my mind on school. I got so far behind in some of my classes that it didn't even pay for me to be there. So I didn't go." He shrugged his shoulders and laughed.

It was that laugh that did it for me. "How can you laugh about anything so serious, Lenny? It's your whole life you're ruining! Are you too dumb to see it, or is it that you just don't care?" Furiously, I stood up and gathered my books, ready to storm out of the candy store.

He grabbed my arm to stop me. "Hold on a minute, Linda! There are a few things I want to say to you before you go storming out of here. First of all, since this is my report card, I shouldn't have to bother explaining it to you. But I do want you to understand something, so I'm going to try. Just because you find it easy to do well in school doesn't mean that everyone else does."

I sat back down. "I know that, Lenny. Some people aren't as smart as others, or maybe they have learning disabilities or something. But that's not the case here. You don't have any problems learning what you want to know, and you're every bit as smart as I am. If I can do well in school, you should be able to, too!"

"That sounds like it should be the case, but it's not," he stated. "You can't possibly understand what it's like to be me, Linda. Your house is nice and calm and normal. Your father goes to work all day; your mother has a part-time job and still manages to clean and cook for you. You might argue with your parents, but you still talk to each other like human beings most of the time. You don't know what it does to you when each time you go home you know you'll find somebody screaming like a lunatic, throwing things, breaking things, or pulling knives. You don't know what it's like to have your stomach always tied up in painful knots, worrying what to expect next."

He took a deep breath. "Sometimes I feel like a caged animal. I tried disciplining myself to study, but I can't seem to do it. My mind keeps focusing on the horrors that happened at home or projecting the next horror that's bound to happen. I can feel this terror start to take over my body. The only way to escape it is to escape from what I'm doing and focus on something that's fun. So I leave my house or I leave school. I go get something to eat; I shoot pool; I hang out with my friends. I block out the pain that's eating away at my stomach. It doesn't matter that I might be ruining my future by not doing well in school. The first thing I've got to do is get through the day; in fact, to get through these moments when I'm so full of turmoil I think I'm going to explode!"

He looked at me with eyes full of anguish. "Sure, it's easy to see me from the outside and make the judgment that I'm doing the wrong thing; there's no doubt about it. You'd have to feel what I'm feeling inside to realize I'm doing the best I can under the circumstances. And that's something I'd never wish on you or anyone else—to feel what it's like to be me."

I tried hard to digest what Lenny was saying. In all the time we had been going together, I had never realized the extent to which the turmoil of his home life affected him. Usually, he would just make jokes about the crazy things that went on at home. I had been totally unaware that this could keep him from doing what he should in school. I had been judging him without knowing the facts.

I felt so guilty that I could feel tears welling up in my eyes. "I'm sorry, Lenny. I didn't understand how tough it was for you. I'm not mad about your report card any longer, really I'm not. But something's got to be done to turn it around for you in school. What do you think it should be?"

He sighed: "I'll have to try harder, I guess. Keep out of my house more. Study with you in the afternoons. I'll do better this term; I know I will. Especially if you're going to be coming to Washington next year—that'll really give me an incentive!"

"Good!" I said. But then I thought of something not so good. "What about the bowling team, Lenny? How are you going to get them to let you stay on it?"

"I'm not. I already got the notice that I'm being booted off because of the drop in my grades. Imagine! They're letting Fran, who can barely throw the ball straight, stay on the team because her average is up there, and I get kicked off even though I'm the best bowler on the team. Well, I'm not going to let it get to me. It's more important that I spend the time getting my grades back up, right?'' He gave a questioning little smile.

I smiled back, clasped his hand, and gave it a squeeze. "Right!" I answered, for at that moment I believed he meant it. Besides, I loved Lenny so much that I had no choice but to accept his lousy report card. I certainly didn't want to break up with him because of it. And if he could get through the next term without any major disasters, I was sure that things would get better once I started going to Washington with him.

That is, if I could convince my parents to let me go!

Chapter

Twelve

Surprisingly enough, my parents only put up minor opposition to my changing schools. They didn't like the fact that I would be graduating from an ordinary school like Washington instead of a prestigious one like Tech, but they did agree that I would get more out of taking college-level courses in a college rather than staying an extra year in high school. So, with reluctance, they agreed to let me transfer.

"I hope it's for the reasons you told us," my mother said, the day I was to meet with a Washington guidance counselor to arrange the transfer. I had gotten excused early from Tech in order to take care of everything. "I'd hate to think you're transferring just to go to school with that boy."

"His name is Lenny, Ma." I sighed. Would my parents ever come to accept Lenny? "If I were going to transfer because of him, I would have done it a lot sooner.''

Despite what I told my mother, I could feel my heart beating faster as I opened the door to Washington, and I knew full well it was because this was Lenny's school. And Lenny was such a character, such a wise-mouth and a troublemaker, that almost all the students and faculty knew who he was. It made me feel special to go to Washington and be Lenny Lipoff's girlfriend.

Although I hadn't told Lenny what time I would be arriving, he was right there outside the guidance office when I located it. Seeing him, I felt a surge of joy.

''Say hello to Mrs. Randall for me,'' Lenny laughed when I told him with whom I had an appointment. ''She knows me all too well, but she's nice . . . and competent, too—something you won't find much around here.''

Mrs. Randall was very nice—a large, warm-hearted black woman who knew how to make kids feel at ease and that she really cared. She laughed when I told her Lenny said hello, and she told me she was glad my association with him hadn't affected my grades. She checked my courses and came up with a tentative schedule for next year that would enable me to graduate easily. All I had to do was to get my parents to sign their approval, get Tech to release my records, then bring my final report card to Mrs. Randall, and she would have everything set for me to start Washington as a senior in September.

''I can hardly believe it—I'm actually going to

skip eleventh grade!" I told Lenny joyfully as I walked to the bus with him, Billy, Nicky, Fran, and Jessie after school. It was as wonderful as I had imagined—to be at the same school as my boyfriend and my friends from the neighborhood.

I wasn't the only one with good news. When we got on the bus, Jessie reported that Sheldon's mother had been speaking to her mother on the phone a good deal recently. Mrs. Scaley had connections with the manager of the building where they lived. She knew of someone moving out of a three-bedroom apartment on the fifth floor, and had been trying to get it for Mrs. Emory. Now it looked as if she had been successful. Mrs. Emory had decided she didn't like her new neighborhood nearly as much as Washington Heights. Sheldon was always coming back on weekends anyway. She had given up her fight to keep him away from the influences of his friends. If all went well, Sheldon would be moving into Jessie's building at the end of the month!

"Score one for our crowd!" Lenny yelled when he heard this. "Victory over all those who attempt to tear us apart!"

At this, all the kids on the bus cheered loudly. The rest of the passengers looked at us as if we were crazy, but we didn't care. It felt too good to be young and part of a crowd, and have things going our way for a change. I couldn't wait until I could finally transfer to Washington!

Once Sheldon moved into Jessie's building, the two of them became a couple. Since he and Lenny were best friends, the four of us wound up going out together pretty often.

As strange as it was to see Sheldon with a girl other than Roz, I was glad that Lenny and I had another couple to go out with. Of course, it wasn't the same as it had been when Sheldon was dating Roz; I could never have with Jessie what I had had with her.

Jessie was a lot of fun when she wanted to be, but she was also moody and could snap at you at the least provocation. But what really stood between us was the fact that Jessie tended to lie a lot. I never knew if she was giving me a truthful answer to a question, and I was never able to get that close to a person whom I couldn't really trust. As a result, my relationship with Jessie was friendly, but very superficial. I couldn't tell her the kinds of things I used to share with Roz and Fran, and even, at one time, with Donna.

Still, it was fun to go out on couples' dates with Sheldon and Jessie. Since Jessie's parents were divorced and her mother worked long hours, her apartment was often available to us if we needed someplace to hang out or make out without being disturbed. And Sheldon was much less resentful of Lenny's relationship with me since he acquired his own girlfriend. So, having Sheldon and Jessie as a couple was definitely a positive step. The longer we went out together, the more fun we all seemed to have.

One Sunday afternoon, we went roller skating. We had a great time chasing each other, bumping into one another, and making a chain and whipping the end person around. It was especially funny when Lenny, who was a great speed skater, had let go when he was end man in the chain. He had taken off so fast that he had to dodge around six people to prevent a major collision, and he wound up falling flat on his rear end with his legs sticking up.

We were still laughing about how ridiculous he had looked when we got off the bus, back in our neighborhood. We were laughing so hard that I didn't notice Roz, who was walking on the opposite side of the street from us, until she was well up the block. I was about to call after her, but thought better of it. Maybe Roz would feel uncomfortable facing the four of us now that Sheldon was with Jessie. There was a chance she hadn't even seen us, so I figured it would be best to leave well enough alone and say nothing.

Seeing Roz made me realize that it had been weeks since we had last spoken to one another. I still liked Roz as much as ever, but we didn't have as much in common as we used to. She wasn't very interested in what I did with Lenny, and I didn't even know her friends from Fine Arts. Still, there were other things we used to talk about—how we felt about school or parents or our futures or kids we both knew—so that wasn't the reason we had stopped calling each other. I wondered if we both felt funny about the fact that Sheldon, Jessie, Lenny, and I were a foursome now. I didn't want that to stand in the way of our friendship. I made up my mind to call her that night.

I tried her once, but her line was busy. Then Lenny came over, and we got involved in doing homework together. I was so glad to see him really trying that I didn't want to leave him in order to call Roz. I figured the call could wait until the next day.

The next day was Monday, and my last class was cancelled, so I decided to go home. It was probably because I was on the train earlier than usual that I happened to spot Roz at the other end of the car.

Great, I thought happily. This would give me the chance to talk to her in person, which was better than a phone call. I started making my way toward her. "Hi, Roz!" I raised my hand in friendly greeting as I saw her look my way.

But instead of greeting me back, Roz shot me a look of such intense anger and dislike that it stopped me in my tracks. Before I could say another word, she turned her back to me, pulled open the door at the end of the car, and walked through it to the next one.

She couldn't have hurt me more if she had slapped me. My face burned with embarrassment, and I had to blink back unwanted tears. I realized then that Roz must have seen me with Sheldon and Jessie and was probably upset by it. She was probably upset because I hadn't called her recently as well. But she hadn't called me, either, and I wasn't angry, and it certainly wasn't my fault that Sheldon was dating Jessie. Roz and I had been friends for so long; I didn't understand how she could treat me this way.

I was so upset at being snubbed by Roz, that I headed straight for the Washington bus stop the moment I got off the train. I couldn't wait to talk to

Lenny about what had happened. He would know what to say to make me feel better.

I watched hopefully as his usual bus unloaded. Most of the kids from the crowd were there, but Lenny wasn't. "Where's Lenny?" I asked Billy.

"Beats me." He shrugged. "He was in school this morning; I saw him. He was all upset about something. But he didn't show up at the cafeteria for lunch. I figured maybe he didn't feel well and went home."

I didn't wait to talk to anyone else. If Lenny went home, he probably was really sick. He didn't like to be around the house during the day if his uncle was there and likely to cause a scene. I ran the five blocks to Lenny's house to see what was the matter. I rang the doorbell, heedless of the fact that Uncle Art was the one most likely to answer.

As I feared, Uncle Art opened the door. I could tell he was drunk right away because he smelled like alcohol and could hardly stand up straight. "Is Lenny home?" I asked timidly.

"You just missed 'im," Art slurred his reply. "I sent him to the store to get me li'l somethin'. He'll be right back. Why don'cha come in and wait for him?"

I hesitated. The last thing I wanted to do was be alone in the house with Uncle Art when he had been drinking. But as I tried to come up with a reply that wouldn't hurt his feelings, he grabbed my arm and pulled me inside. "Come on in. I've somethin' I want to talk to you about. It's important."

Art must have noticed the fear on my face because he started to laugh as he led me into the living room. "There's nothin' to be afraid of here, sweety. Sit down."

I plopped down on the chair farthest from the sofa where Art sat. "Yes?" I asked.

"Well, you're a nice girl, sweety, and that's why I want you to know the truth before it's too late. My nephew is no good for you, no good at all. He's just like his mother. You can't trust him or believe a word he tells you. He'll sweet-talk you into doing anythin' for him, and when he's got you where he wants you—boom! He'll deflate you as if you were a balloon. Then it'll be too late for you, baby. All over. You're gone!"

I listened to this jumble of words with a sense of horror. How could Lenny's uncle talk to me this way? He had no right to say those awful things to me about Lenny. The man was crazy and drunk besides. I shouldn't have come in to listen to him. I should have known better. All I wanted to do now was get away from him before he said anything to make me feel worse. But I had to be careful how I did it. It would be all too easy to set him off into one of the rages Lenny had told me about.

Slowly, I got up from the chair. "Well, thank you very much for the advice, sir. But I really think I should wait for Lenny outside. I have to—"

"Sid down!" His authoritative order had me back in my seat in no time. "I'm not finished with what I have to tell you," he said with a sadistic grin. "And it's somethin' I'm sure you'll want to know."

"W-what?"

"I got a call from the principal of Lenny's school today—they thought I was his father." Art gave a nasty laugh, and then continued with renewed clarity to his voice. "He told me that they had caught Lenny cutting second period and were furious because they had caught him doing the same thing on Friday. They sent him back to class with a warning that they were sick of the disturbances and bad influence he created in school. They told him that the next time he was caught cutting, that would be it for him. They would ask no questions but throw him out of school."

"Oh, no! How awful! He—"

"Just hold it, sister! This story's not over." Uncle Art laughed his evil laugh. "You know what your precious boyfriend did next? He waited all the way to third period to see if he could beat the system. He was caught trying to leave the building by a side entrance. And the principal stuck to his word, too. Lenny Lipoff is no longer a student at Washington High School. He's out for good!"

"No! It can't be true! I don't believe you!" I stood up and shook my head vehemently. "They wouldn't do that to Lenny! He's too smart! They wouldn't!"

As I said this, I heard the key turn in the door, and Lenny came inside. He was carrying a carton of cigarettes, which he would never get for his uncle unless he was under tremendous pressure. I could tell by the look on his face that this pressure was something far beyond what usually went on in his house. I knew then that what his uncle had told me was true.

As this realization hit me, I was overwhelmed by the magnitude of it all. Lenny was thrown out of school! There were no more chances, no more opportunities to get it together, to make it up next term. We would never go to school together, have lunch in the cafeteria, ride back together on the bus. Lenny's high school career was over, terminated at age seventeen. What kind of future would he have without an education? What kind of future could we have together if he didn't go to school?

It was too much for me to deal with, too much for me to face up to right now. I had to get away from Lenny, his horrible house, and his drunken uncle. I brushed by Lenny so fast he didn't have time to stop me. "Your uncle told me about school," was all I said to him as I raced out into the hall.

"Linda! Wait! We've got to talk about this!" he called after me.

He was right of course, but I couldn't handle it now. I had to be alone, to think this out by myself.

I couldn't go home, where Lenny would expect to find me and where my mother was sure to notice something was wrong. Instead, I turned the corner and headed in the opposite direction, toward the Hudson River. I walked past the wall where Lenny and I had first gotten together, where we had spent so many romantic summer nights watching the sun set behind the river and the great steel bridge. The river was cold now, gray and barren, strewn with chunks of floating ice. The biting wind whipped off the water and made me shiver. It stung my cheeks and froze the tip of my nose. My eyes began to water, but whether from the cold outside or the pain inside, I didn't know.

And I didn't care. Lenny was thrown out of school. It was over. And no doubt it should be over with us, too. To stay with him now meant I would only get more deeply involved with him, so deep I might never be able to let go. I could predict nothing but problems ahead for me and Lenny. There was so much we had to overcome.

Yet I loved him so much that the thought of breaking up with him was unbearable to me. What was I going to do?

Chapter
Thirteen

I was so mixed up that I still wasn't ready to speak to Lenny when he called me that night. "I can't talk to you about it yet," was all I said before slamming down the phone.

It rang again. "Look, Lenny, I told you. I'm just not ready to talk yet. I'm too upset and too confused." I hung up again.

This happened two more times. My parents started to protest and grumble. By the fifth time the phone rang, they had all they could take. "You tell that boy to stop calling here," my mother said angrily. "We're entitled to some peace in this house!"

I realized the only way to get peace was if I agreed to talk to Lenny. So I reluctantly made up to meet him at our usual spot in the candy store after he got off work.

When I arrived, he was already there, sitting in our favorite back booth. We had sat there so many times, sharing food, talking, holding hands, gazing into each other's eyes. Now the only thing I saw in his eyes were anguish and pain.

It saddened me to see him like that. Even though I had been hurt by what he had done, I realized it was himself he had hurt the most. I decided to be as easy on him as possible. "Well," I said. "Do you want to tell me what happened?"

"Not really," he admitted. "But I will." He took a deep breath. "I guess it started with the fight in my house last night. This one began with the usual screaming between my mother and uncle, but it soon changed its focus to me. One moment, each one was yelling that the other was no good; the next moment they were both yelling that I was no good. Nothing unusual for them, except this time my uncle went too far. He ran into my room, where I was attempting to escape from their lunacy by listening to some records, and began to rant that I did nothing but blast my stereo all day. Then, without warning, he grabbed a handful of records and began smashing them against the wall."

Lenny's eyes flashed with anger at the memory. "This was more than I could take. I went to pull the remaining records out of my uncle's hand. He whirled around to get away from me and wound up hitting my mother across the face with the records. Instead of taking it out on him, she chose to vent her anger on the records, and she smashed the ones he hadn't been able to break.

"By this time we were all so furious that there's

no way to describe the insane scene that followed. Everyone was pulling and shoving and screaming. I demanded my uncle get out of our house; he refused; my mother stuck up for him because he supposedly was on the verge of finding a good job and she expects him to give her some money; I yelled that she always put money ahead of everything. It got so crazy that I had to get out of there. I spent the night in the poolroom and was really exhausted in the morning." He paused, and I sat holding my breath, waiting for him to go on.

"I made it through first period at school, but by second period, I thought I was going to go out of my mind. I was so exhausted, and scenes from the night before kept running through my head. I felt as if I would burst if I didn't get out of school and get some air. I was so upset I didn't take my usual precautions, and I was caught by Mr. Kinney, the dean. I guess he decided to make an example out of me, because he took me straight to the principal, who told me that this was my last warning, and I'd be kicked out of school the next time I got caught cutting.

"I guess I didn't fully believe him; but even if I had, I don't think I could have sat through another class. I was so distraught I left the office and headed straight for a side door I knew about. Kinney must have followed me or something, because he nabbed me right away. He took me back to the principal, who called home, spoke to my uncle, and told him I was out. That's all there was to it." Lenny shook his head miserably. "Except for the additional crap

I had to face when I got home and how it's affecting you.''

By this time, listening to Lenny's story, I found all anger had left me. What remained was an over-whelming sadness for all his problems that I couldn't fix. It wasn't his fault that he had been born into such an unstable family. If I had grown up in a home like his, I don't know if I could have concentrated on school either. Listening to his story and understanding his pain made me realize how much I loved him for all the good traits he had despite his problems—his warmth, his depth, his feeling and caring, his common sense, the humor he injected into everything, and his ability to keep on trying no matter how many things went wrong— I couldn't abandon him now that life had given him such a severe blow. I would stick with him through this horrible time, and somehow, it would get better again.

I reached out and clasped his hand. "Oh, Lenny. This is so awful. What do you think you can do now?"

"I've been thinking about that all day. The answer is obvious. If I could move out of my house now I'd do it in a minute, but I can't. I'm too young, and I don't have enough money to make it by myself. So I've got to stand living at home a while longer. I'm going to go downtown tomorrow and look for a full-time job. I know I can't make much to start with, but I'll look for something with a future. I'm smart, and I know I can learn faster while working than I can in school. I'll register for night school so that I can eventually get my diploma. It might take me longer, but I can do it if I try. Besides, between a full-time job and night school, I won't be home much. I might have to live there, but the less time I spend there the better. Who knows? Maybe, in the long run, this will even turn out to be a good thing for me." He gave me a tentative little smile.

I couldn't smile back yet, but I did give his hand a squeeze of encouragement. That was to let him know that as long as he kept trying, I'd be right there with him.

True to his word, Lenny found a job that very week. It was only an entry-level clerk's position and didn't pay much, but it was in an accounting office. Lenny was good with figures, and he hoped to get enough experience on the job to learn accounting. He was very positive about the job.

He also started night school, and I was pleasantly surprised by his reaction. "It's much better for me than day school. The teachers recognize that the students are adults and are there because they want to be. They don't treat us like babies—it's wonderful!"

As he had hoped, another good thing about Lenny's new routine was that he had little time to spend at home. I would meet him after work at the subway station, and we would walk back to my house together. We would sit in my hallway on the steps between the second and third floor landings, and talk and make out. Then Lenny would get something to eat in a fast-food restaurant and go straight to night school. He didn't have to have any contact with his mother and uncle until he came home late at night. If he was lucky, they would be watching TV or sleeping, and he could go to his room without dealing with them.

I missed spending the afternoons with Lenny, but I realized it had to be this way. We still had the time together after he came home from work, and we still had the weekends. Sometimes we would do things with some of the other kids from the crowd; sometimes we would go out with Sheldon and Jessie, or by ourselves. Because I didn't see Lenny during the afternoons, I sometimes found myself going home after school with Cesca. We became close enough to partially fill the void caused by the fact that I now never saw Roz and had only occasional contact with Fran and Donna.

So, in general, things were better than I expected them to be the first couple of months after Lenny got kicked out of school. My parents, of course, were distraught when they heard what had happened and put enormous pressure on me to break up with him. I told them flat out that I loved Lenny, and the only way we would break up was if he decided to do so. Of course, after all we had come through together, I never expected this might come to pass.

Then the first signs of spring made their appearance, bringing longer days, warmer weather, and the wonderful sights and smells of new growth bursting through sun-baked earth. Spring made me fell especially romantic. I wanted nothing more than to walk through the park hand in hand with Lenny, to share the miracles of the season with him. But, instead, I started feeling subtle vibrations of resistance and resentment from him.

It started with his canceling a few weekend plans we had made with various excuses that didn't seem quite valid. When he did go out with me, he rushed me home earlier than usual so he'd have time to spend hanging out with the boys afterward. And then he began complaining about his situation at work.

Suddenly, the job no longer seemed to have the promise and potential he thought it would have. The bosses were taking advantage of him and assigning him all these menial jobs to do. He was upset; he was annoyed; he was cranky when he came home from work. As a result, he often snapped at and took his frustrations out on me. Then, one Friday afternoon, he showed up at Bronx Tech to ride home with me on the subway.

"What are you doing here?" I gasped when I saw him. "You're supposed to be at work!"

"Not anymore," he laughed. "I quit the job today!"

"You quit?" I said in horror. "But why?"

He had a list of reasons. "I wasn't being taught the things they promised they'd teach me. I didn't get the raise they said they'd give me after two months. But worst of all, they treated me as if I were some sort of servant. When they ordered me to clean out their dirty ashtrays, I had all I could take. I see enough filthy ashtrays at home thanks to my mother and uncle. I wasn't going to clean those out for anyone!"

"But Lenny, you can't tell an employer what you

do and don't want to do. Especially in the beginning. You've got to accept what goes with the job!''

"Oh, no I don't. There are plenty of other jobs out there, and I'll find one where they treat me like a human being.''

"But shouldn't you—I mean wouldn't it have been better if you had waited to quit until you found something else?''

"Should have, would have, could have!'' he scoffed. "It's all meaningless speculation. I guess I quit in a fit of anger, but now that I did, I'm glad! I'll find something better, and in the meanwhile I need a vacation. It's hard going to work all day, and to night school, too!''

"I know. But you're the one who got yourself into this situation, and you've got to handle it.''

This was not what Lenny wanted to hear. He started yelling at me that I always had something to say about things I knew nothing about, and the least I could do was be happy he had come all the way out to Tech to ride home with me.

I answered that I would be happy if only he had some good news to tell me for a change, and would he please lower his voice because he was making a scene on the train.

He raised his voice even louder, stating he didn't care about the nosy people on the train, and if all I could do was criticize him, maybe we'd be better off not seeing so much of each other.

I hotly replied it was fine with me if that was the way he wanted it.

"It is,'' he said. He calmly got up and walked to

the next car of the train, leaving me there with all my pent-up fury.

I was tempted to run after him and vent some more anger, but thought better of it. I was embarrassed enough by the scene we had just played out on the train. There were kids I knew from Tech riding there, and I still had to face them for the rest of the year. I decided to wait until we got off at our stop to talk to him further.

But Lenny was not among those who got off the train at our station. I stood there, my eyes scanning the platform, until the last person disappeared up the staircase. Then I realized he probably stayed on the train an extra stop so he could get off closer to the poolroom. There he could always find some other bum who wasn't working or going to school to hang out with. It was just like him to escape to the poolroom instead of working on a way to make his situation better!

Well, let him, I told myself. I had had about as much of Lenny, his problems, and his instability as I could handle right now. Maybe it was time for me to let go of him and take a look at some of the other boys who were available, boys who didn't have all of Lenny's complications.

Despite my conviction that I'd be better off without Lenny, I was miserable spending Friday night without him. I tried to interest myself in the TV program my brothers were watching and in the latest book I had gotten out of the library, but there was no way I could concentrate on either. My mind kept drifting back to him and wondering what he was doing. Was he hanging around the poolroom or cutting loose somewhere with the boys, or was he spiteful enough to be doing something that involved girls as well?

It didn't take me too long to find out. It was about nine o'clock, and I had just thrown my book down in frustration after what seemed like the hundredth unsuccessful attempt to get involved in the story, when the telephone rang. I ran to get it, hoping it would be Lenny, ready to make up, but it wasn't. It was Jessie Scaley.

"Are you sitting down, Linda?" she asked.

"I am now," I replied, taking the phone into the hall closet and plopping down on a blanket-padded area I had made in one corner. It was the only place in my apartment I could have a private conversation. "Why?"

"Because you're not going to like the news I have to tell you. Do you know where Sheldon and Lenny are tonight?"

"No. Lenny and I had a fight this afternoon. I haven't seen or heard from him since."

"Oh, how convenient!" Jessie said sarcastically. "It just so happens that Sheldon picked a fight with me, too, and over nothing. I had this feeling he did it so he wouldn't have to see me tonight because he had something else planned. So I looked out the window until I saw him leave the building. Then I followed him from a distance to see where he would go. Guess where that was?"

"The poolroom?" I attempted.

"Wrong. He stopped and waited by the entrance to the subway. It didn't take me long to find whom he was waiting for, either. Lenny, Joel Fudd, and Louie Fields all showed up within minutes of one another. They were all nicely dressed and had their hair neatly combed. They looked too good to be going to the poolroom. And since Joel and Louie are two of the biggest lover-boys in the neighborhood, I knew right away that wherever they were going involved girls.''

"I bet you're right," I gasped.

"I am right. As soon as they left I went right up to Sheldon's house to talk to his mother. She and I have gotten pretty close since they moved into my building. She likes me because she thinks I'm a good influence on Sheldon. I make him study more and run around less. She told me the boys were heading out to Queens to go to a party with some girls Louie knew through his cousin.''

"A party? With girls from Queens? Why, those dirty, rotten, double-crossing—"

"My sentiments exactly," Jessie interrupted. "Just because Sheldon and I aren't officially going steady doesn't mean it's right for him to do something underhanded like pick a fight with me so he can go off to a party with other girls. I have half a mind to break up with him altogether!''

"That's the way I feel," I agreed. Only worse, I thought. Jessie and Sheldon had only been going together a short time. Lenny and I would be together two years in July—if we made it that long. We had been through so much together, and I had been there for him through all the disasters in school and at home. This type of sneaky action was the kind of thing I might have expected him to do last year when our relationship was so unstable; I thought we had matured to the point where we were past all that now. Despite the fact that I had been entertaining thoughts of breaking up with Lenny myself, I was crushed by what Jessie had told me. Absolutely crushed.

I stayed up half the night thinking about Lenny at this party with other girls. What if he met someone there he liked more than me? My insides churned with jealousy at the mere thought.

Even though we had an agreement that we could each date others if we wanted to, since we had gone back together neither of us had done so. If Lenny had wanted to see someone else, the right thing would have been for him to have come to me and said so. Sneaking off to this party behind my back was, as Jessie had said, an underhanded thing to do.

The other half of the night was spent trying to decide the best way to confront Lenny with what I had found out. Should I attack him outright for being such a sneak; should I act hurt and indignant; should I rise above the situation and pretend it didn't matter; should I make a stand and break up with him once and for all? I kept vacillating from favoring one approach to another. I didn't know what to do.

I fell asleep so late that most of the morning was gone by the time I awakened. It took me a while to recall the reason for the sick feeling that enveloped me. I still hadn't decided what to do about Lenny. I was tempted to go to his house and drag him out of bed, but I didn't want to face his mother or his uncle.

Instead, I decided to go to the park. It was such a beautiful day that Lenny was bound to show up there sooner or later. I could decide what to do when I saw him.

I called Jessie and asked her to meet me at the back of the park with her racquetball equipment. The racquetball courts were located to one side of the baseball field, so we would be able to spot the boys when they arrived and still give the appearance of being busy and unconcerned.

It was pretty hard to concentrate on racquetball while keeping a constant lookout for the boys. Finally, our persistence paid off when we saw them approaching the batter's cage. They were carrying their baseball gloves and obviously intended to get into the game.

"Don't look at them, Jessie," I whispered to her. "Let's see if they come over to us."

Jessie and I directed our attention to the ball that came bouncing off the wall as if it were the most important thing in our lives. She hit it, and I raced after it as fast as I could. I was so intent on the ball that I didn't notice Lenny had arrived on the court until I went crashing into him. We both went flying to the ground.

"Why don't you look where you're going?" he demanded, shoving me off him angrily.

"What are you doing in the middle of our game, anyhow?" I retorted, scrambling to my feet and brushing myself off.

He stood up, looking all indignant. "I came to

talk to you—on the remote chance that you might have calmed down since our last meeting.''

"If I had calmed down? I believe it was you who stalked off the train.''

"Oh, stop this childish bickering over nonsense,'' Jessie said as she and Sheldon came over to where Lenny and I were standing, glaring at each other. "Let's get down to the real issues here, Linda. Like the party they went to last night.''

Sheldon and Lenny looked at each other; then they looked over at Jessie and me. "How did you find out about the party?'' asked Sheldon.

"Never mind how we found out,'' Jessie replied. "The point is that we're wise to your game of picking fights with us so you can go off and cheat on us with other girls. And we're not going to put up with it any longer.''

"No?'' Sheldon and Lenny both laughed. "And what do you intend to do about it?'' demanded Lenny. "Lock us up in our rooms and put the keys in your pocketbooks?''

"Don't be such a wise guy, Lenny,'' I said. "No one wants to lock anyone up. We all have agreements we can go out with whomever we please. But that doesn't mean you should do it by picking a fight and sneaking out behind our backs. That's not the right way to handle it.''

"Is that so? Well, how do you expect me to handle it, Linda?'' Lenny's face started getting red and the veins in his neck began to stick out the way they did when he got mad. "You don't know how difficult it is to tell you anything you don't like. Look how crazy you got when I told you I quit my job—something that shouldn't even concern you. You would have flipped out if I had told you I was going to the party. That's why I didn't say anything.''

"That's complete bull!" I retorted hotly. "You didn't tell me because you felt guilty, so you made up the excuse that I wouldn't handle it right. You conveniently do this every time you do something wrong."

"Well, it wasn't wrong to go to this party. It was great. I met some girls there who know how to appreciate me. They didn't carry on about every little thing I might have done wrong. They were sweet and nice and grateful for my attentions. They knew how to act like ladies—not like you!"

When Lenny said this, it was like pushing a button in my brain. These were the same kinds of things he had said to me last year when he broke up with me—that other girls were better than I was and knew how to act like ladies. It was only after he went out with them that he realized they, too, had faults, and that I was the one he liked best. I thought he had learned that lesson, but here he was, saying the same thing all over again. It hurt, and it made me positively furious!

"Well, if that's how you feel, Lenny, after all this time, why don't we just forget it?" I sputtered. "You can go have your wonderful Queens girls who act like ladies. You certainly don't need lowly me anymore!"

"It is the way I feel, and that's why I made a date with one of them, Janice, for tonight. So now you can't accuse me of doing this behind your back.

Janice and I hit it off really well. I'm taking her out tonight and as many times as I want to after that. That's all there is to it!''

"Fine. That's all there is to it!" I turned on my heel and stalked across the ball field to exit from the park, oblivious to the shouts to get off the field because I was ruining the game.

I was too angry to care what anyone said to me. Too angry and too hurt.

I couldn't believe this was happening. One day I had a boyfriend who was trying to do the right thing with his life, and who told me he loved me. The next day I find he quit his job and wanted to take out other girls.

I turned around and saw Lenny was laughing with Sheldon as if they had just shared something extremely funny. It made me even angrier to see him taking the end of our relationship as one big joke!

It was a good thing I felt both the anger and the disbelief, part of me realized. They were good tools to keep me from really feeling the pain. That, I knew, was bound to set in soon enough.

Chapter

Fourteen

Jessie and I stayed together all that afternoon, giving each other moral support. At night, we got together with Kathy and Donna and some of the other girls in the neighborhood, and we all went out to a movie. I tried hard to have a good time, but I couldn't help thinking about Lenny sitting in a movie in Queens with that Janice. Would he have his arm around her? Would he be kissing her? Would he be telling her how glad he was to have found her, to have broken away from me?

I worked myself into such a state with these thoughts that I was a total wreck by the time I got home. Thankful that my parents already seemed to be asleep, I threw myself on my bed and let the full extent of my misery take over.

And take over it did. Thoughts of how it had been when Lenny and I were good together flooded my mind. Pictures of the two of us—walking hand in hand through the park, sitting gazing into one another's eyes in the candy store, making out in the hallway, being so much in love—came and went. I heard him say the wonderful things he used to say to me: how no girl had more depth or feeling or understanding than I did; how he loved to be with me more than with anyone else; even, what it might be like someday if we were married.

And then I thought of what he had done and said that obliterated the good things that had come before: the "I don't care" look on his face when he told me he quit his job; stalking off and leaving me on the subway; going to the party behind my back; telling me he had met another girl who was better than I was and that he was taking her out from now on.

It was over. All the wonderful things that Lenny and I had had together were now in the past. In their place was a gaping void that stretched in front of me like an empty nightmare.

It was over. Icy fingers of pain grabbed the inside of my stomach and rose to my chest until I found it impossible to breathe. I gasped for air, hoping for relief, but there was none available.

It was only after what seemed like hours of crying into my pillow that I managed to fall into a fitful, restless sleep.

The pain was with me when I woke up the next morning. It got worse when I received a call from Jessie, informing me she had made up with Sheldon. He had already gotten bored with the Queens girls and had been waiting for her when she came back from the movies. He had promised her he wouldn't go to those parties anymore. Lenny, however, was another story. Sheldon had told Jessie that Lenny was making out with Janice all evening long.

The thought of it made me so sick I couldn't eat anything for breakfast. Naturally, my parents noticed and questioned me until, out of a need to talk to someone, I told them what had happened.

Surprisingly enough, they were sympathetic. After a few expected remarks like, "We knew that boy would only bring you pain," they started trying to encourage me.

"You have so much going for you, Linda. Start seeing your friends again. Go out, have fun, and meet new people. You'll find there are plenty of other boys out there if you only give yourself a chance. You might feel as if your life is over now, but there are wonderful things ahead of you. The sooner you make up your mind to forget that boy, the sooner things will start going your way!"

Although I was too miserable then to accept what my parents told me, their words made an impression. I stayed in the house, feeling sorry for myself, until I couldn't stand it anymore. I realized I had to get out, to work off some energy, or I would drive myself absolutely insane!

Fortunately, the weather was beautiful outside. It was the kind of warm, clear, sun-filled spring day that ordinarily would have made me feel good just to be alive—if only I didn't have this tremendous load weighing heavily on my shoulders. I decided to walk toward Ft. Tryon Park. It was so beautiful there; it had to make me feel better.

Lost in my own thoughts, I walked farther than I had expected. Before I realized it, I had come to the Cloisters, and since it was almost time for the concert to begin, I went to sit in that peaceful courtyard garden where I had once talked to Fran about going back with Lenny. I sat there, listening to the music, thinking of what I might have done differently to keep from losing him. "Hi, Linda!" a voice interrupted my thoughts. "What are you doing here?"

"Fran!" Startled, I jumped to my feet. While Fran and I hadn't had a specific problem like I had with Roz, it had been months now since I had seen her. Our lives had just drifted in different directions since I had become so serious with Lenny, and she had gotten involved with dating different boys. "I'm here to listen to the music."

"Oh. But where's Lenny?"

I felt a fresh stab of pain. "He's not here. We broke up."

"Again? Well, it was bound to happen. The two of you are so different. Truthfully, I was surprised you stayed together as long as you did this time."

"It was really good this time, Fran," I blurted out. "We got so close; we went through so much together. I thought we would make it for sure. And then—and then—he found some new girl in Queens he decided is better than I am and dumped me like some worthless piece of garbage!"

"You poor thing," Fran said sympathetically. "You still haven't learned it's better not to place so much emphasis on anyone. You've got to be your own person, be independent, date lots of boys. Then none of them has the power to hurt you. Look, I'm supposed to meet Roz and a couple of boys she knows from Fine Arts here. Why don't you stick around and we'll introduce them to you.''

"Roz? Boys? Oh, no—I couldn't! I mean, the boys are for you and her; you don't need me to interfere. And besides, Roz is mad at me."

"The boys are just friends, so don't worry about interfering with anything. As for Roz, she's not mad at you, just at the way you removed yourself from us because of your all-consuming relationship with Lenny. Here she is now. Hey, Roz! Look who I found here—Linda! And she finally broke up with Lenny.''

I was relieved to see Roz smile. "Well, it's about time you returned to the human race, Linda. Welcome back to the world!''

My initial reaction was to be angry at Roz's words, especially after she had snubbed me in the subway. But, when I thought about it, I could see why she felt that way. When I was going with Lenny I got so involved with him it was as if no one else mattered. In a sense, breaking up with him did mean I was returning to the world, certainly as far as my friendship with Roz was concerned. Even though I didn't like the way she chose to go about it, I realized Roz had only been trying to get that message across to me. With that thought, all anger melted away. "Good to see you, Roz," I said tentatively.

"Good to see you, too," she grinned. "Do you

remember Peter and Julian?'' She indicated the two boys who were standing behind her. ''They came into Nick's the night we were there with Sheldon and Lenny.''

''Right. The night Sheldon and Lenny acted like first class jerks,'' I recalled.

We all laughed, and after that I didn't feel like an outsider anymore. We listened to the chamber music concert together and then walked through the galleries of the Cloisters. Even though I had seen the artwork before, seeing it now in the company of Peter and Julian made a big difference. They knew so much about the history of the various pieces and the artists who created them; it made the medieval period suddenly come alive. It was so interesting, I hardly thought of Lenny the whole time.

Back in my own bed at night, the aching emptiness took over once again, and I cried myself to sleep. But I woke up Monday morning with a feeling of determination. As miserable as I was over my breakup with Lenny, I didn't have to let it affect every aspect of my life. Take school for example. I made the decision to block out my unhappiness by concentrating as hard as I could on what was going on in school.

At first, it was a struggle. I would try to pay attention to what my history teacher was saying, but the Revolutionary War seemed like nothing compared to the war going on between Lenny and me. And Spanish made me think of all the times I had tried to tutor Lenny in that subject. It wasn't until I got to math, with the moral support from

Cesca sitting next to me, that I found I could concentrate on what the teacher was saying. By the time we sat down to lunch, at our usual table with Mike and Sandy, I was starting to feel a little better.

"Guess what?" Cesca announced before we even got our lunch bags open. "Linda finally broke up with Lenny."

"Again?" Sandy asked cautiously.

"Uh-huh," I nodded. "But this time it's different. He's found someone else, and I found I've had enough."

"Well, if that isn't perfect timing." Mike grinned. He and I had become good friends this year. "This Friday's the afterschool dance here at Tech, and I've asked my friend, Ralph, who goes to private school, to come along. I have a feeling you two might hit it off."

"Thanks, Mike. But I'm not ready for another relationship yet."

"Relationship?" he laughed. "No one's talking about anything serious like that. I just think we could all have some fun together. Keep yourself open, okay, Linda?"

"Okay," I promised. And suddenly, I found myself feeling better.

All week long, Mike kept telling me about his friend, Ralph. Like Mike, Ralph had grown up on City Island. Although a part of New York City, City Island was like a self-contained small town. Ralph had a wise-guy personality and had gotten into trouble in the public schools. His parents had put him into private school so he would get more discipline.

I found myself listening to Mike's stories with an interest that made we wonder about myself. Why did I find it easier to be attracted to boys who got into trouble than to boys who did the right thing? Was it because they were more exciting?

This certainly seemed to be the case when Mike told me that Ralph was going to sneak into Tech so he could attend the dance, which was supposed to be only for students of the school. My heart was racing with anticipation as Mike and I snuck down to a side entrance to let Ralph in. It was pounding with excitement as the three of us boldly strolled into the gym, where the dance was being held, as if we all belonged there.

It wasn't until Ralph had blended in among the crowd of Tech students that I had a chance to really look at him. He was of medium height and build, and very cute. with dark blond hair and vivid blue eyes. I was intrigued by the way those eyes twinkled with mischief and the way his mouth curved into an easy grin.

"Ralph, this is Linda. Linda—Ralph," Mike said, introducing us.

"Want to dance, Linda?" Ralph lost no time in asking.

"Sure, as soon as I catch my breath," I gasped.

"Come on. I'm out of breath, too. We can be breathless together!" Ralph put his arm around me and led me out to the dance floor.

I put my head on his chest and could hear his

heart beating as rapidly as my own. "Our hearts are beating in rhythm," I said.

"What else would you expect?" he grinned. "It means we're on the right wavelength from the start!"

I laughed. Ralph and I were on the right wavelength. I found him easy to talk to. He told me how he and Mike were friends since they were little kids, and that he had an older brother who lived at home and a sister who was already married. "My parents always told me I'm more trouble than my brother and sister put together," he told me. "But that's because they don't understand me. I'm not bad— just looking for a little excitement!"

Although Ralph liked excitement, he certainly seemed a lot more stable than Lenny. His family was intact, and he was still managing to stick with school. Instead of telling me that other girls were better than I was, he had no problem showing that he was interested in me.

We got along so well that day that he asked me to come with him to a big dance at his school. It would be two weeks from Saturday, and Mike would be taking Cesca, so the four of us could go together.

I said yes immediately. Now I would have something to look forward to, with a boy I might be able to like. And this Sunday, I had plans to go to the Metropolitan Museum with Roz, Fran, Peter, and Julian. Even though there was no romantic involvement there, it was nice to have something like that to do with friends.

It showed me that even though I hadn't seen

Lenny since our breakup, even though I knew from Jessie he was still seeing that Janice from Queens, even though I still ached inside every time I thought of him, there was still hope for me.

With or without Lenny, I was still going to be all right.

Chapter

Fifteen

By the time the big dance came around, I had seen Ralph several times. A couple of times we met after school and hung around Tech with Mike and Cesca; once I went to his house, and once he came to mine.

Ralph lived in a wonderful house that had a view of the bay from his upstairs windows. He took me to his room to watch the boats sailing by, and before I knew it he was kissing me, and we were making out.

It was so strange to be making out with someone who wasn't Lenny. At first I was nervous and stiff, but I did like Ralph, and it wasn't long before I began to relax and enjoy the sensations of his kisses.

The day was warm, and the scent of the sea blew through the open window. The breeze rustled the curtains and caressed my skin. Ralph's touch was so soft that if I closed my eyes I couldn't tell if it was he or the breeze that was caressing me. Making out with Ralph was so different from the way it was with Lenny. The intense passion was lacking, but it was still nice. It made me feel good to know I could actually feel something with another boy.

When Ralph came to my house, my mother was absolutely overjoyed to see me with a boy who wasn't Lenny. She practically fell all over Ralph, offering him an assortment of snacks and telling him how happy she was to meet him. Poor Ralph looked confused, as if he didn't know how to respond. I couldn't wait to get him outside.

"Let's take a walk, Ralph. It's too nice to stay indoors," I suggested. But no sooner did we step outside than I spotted Lenny, standing on the corner with a bunch of his friends.

I couldn't believe my timing. I hadn't seen Lenny at all since the day he broke up with me. And now, the one time I had Ralph with me, there was Lenny, standing on the corner as if it belonged to him.

At the sight of him, I was filled with conflicting emotions. My heart pounded, and I knew then that if I had thought I could get him out of my system so easily, I was only fooling myself. Part of me was afraid of what he might say or do in front of Ralph. Part of me was very glad that Ralph was there to show Lenny he wasn't the only one who could attract someone of the opposite sex.

Even though I was glad Lenny had seen Ralph, I knew it would be best to get him away from Lenny as soon as possible. I smiled and waved to the kids on the corner, and then, grabbing Ralph's hand, steered him away in the opposite direction as quickly as possible.

Not quickly enough. "Wow! Look at them go! Aren't they cute? Linda and her latest boyfriend, and holding hands, too! Watch out, boyfriend; you're heading for nothing but trouble. Wait till she gets her clutches on you!" Lenny's taunts rang out as Ralph and I hurried away.

"What's all that about?" Ralph wanted to know.

I sighed. "My ex-boyfriend. I told you about him."

"Yes, but you also told me it was over. If that's the case, why doesn't he leave you alone?"

"He's the type who has to get in the last word," I tried to explain. "He loves to torture people. Just ignore him, and he's bound to shut up."

But Lenny kept up his remarks until we finally rounded the corner and were out of range of his voice. It was a good thing Ralph could laugh about the whole thing. Someone less good-natured would have wanted no part of me after a scene like that.

Lenny's game was plain for me to see. He didn't want me, but he wanted to fix it so no other boy would want me, either. He made me so mad I could scream!

That evening, I received an interesting call from Jessie. She told me she had heard I had a new boyfriend. She wanted to know all about him and asked me all sorts of detailed questions.

I knew right away that Lenny must have gotten Sheldon to put Jessie up to this. I made sure to tell Jessie all sorts of wonderful things about Ralph:

175

how cute he was, how funny, how caring and appreciative of me. I built up how beautiful and romantic it had been to make out with him with the warm sea breezes blowing across our bodies. I built up the relationship until it sounded like something fantastic.

"Being with Ralph makes me wonder how I ever went with Lenny for so long," I concluded. "Lenny never learned how to treat a girl properly. Now that I know what a boyfriend should be like, I feel sorry for that girl in Queens!"

I hung up, laughing to myself at the look I pictured on Lenny's face when Jessie reported all she had learned about Ralph. And as if to prove I was right in my theory that Lenny was now seeking information, he was there hanging around my corner when I arrived home from school the next day. He leaned against a car and grinned his cocky grin.

Again I felt my heart speed up at the sight of him. Darn it! I didn't like to think he could still affect me this way.

"All alone today, Linda? What happened? Did your little punk boyfriend get sick of you already?"

His words got me angry, which was fortunate because that kept me from feeling soft and susceptible to his charms. "I'll have you know that my 'punk boyfriend,' as you call him, has a lot more going for him than you do. He goes to school and manages to keep a part-time job as well. He might not have as much time to hang around as a bum like you, but at least he's doing something with his life!" My eyes flashed with spiteful anger that wanted to hurt—to hurt him the way he had hurt me.

Lenny laughed in that maddening way he had, but for a brief second I could see in his eyes that what I said had indeed hurt. "Well, you're really trying to hit below the belt today, aren't you, Linda? Calling me a bum without even knowing that I've been going on job interviews every day this week. And that it looks as if I've finally found one which I expect will turn out a lot better than the one I had before!"

"Really? Oh, Lenny, I'm so glad! Tell me about it!" I found myself growing all excited at his news. I had to remind myself that we were broken up, and it shouldn't even matter to me whether he had a job or not. It would only give him more money to spend on his new girlfriend.

"It's downtown, for a company that handles computer supplies. It's a good opportunity for me to learn the computer business."

Now it was impossible for me to stay mad at him. "That would be wonderful! And maybe you could take computer courses at school and—"

"Hey, wait a minute! One step at a time. I'm not even sure I've got the job yet. But I went through the first interview fine, and I'm scheduled to meet the top boss on Monday, so it looks good."

"It does!" I smiled at him, and he smiled back at me. I felt an intense magnetic pull drawing me to him, the way it always had. I was so defenseless against Lenny. Why did he continue to affect me this way no matter how much hurt he inflicted upon me?

I forced my eyes away from his. "So, what else

is going on with you? What's happening with your uncle?''

"There may be more good news there, too. He finally heard from one of the companies he sent his résumés to. They've offered him a job. The best part is that it's in Washington, so he'll have to move away if he takes it. He had the interview yesterday, and he actually managed to show up sober, so he should be out soon.''

"That's great. And what about your mother?''

"She's so thrilled to be getting rid of my uncle that she's been almost human to me.''

"Well, it looks as if you're finally starting to get your life in order, then. Maybe all you needed was to get away from me and find a new girlfriend," I said bitterly.

"That's not it at all. I got serious about looking for a job because I knew I had to do something with myself, and the thing with my uncle just happened. As for Janice, she's just a girl I've been seeing, not really my girlfriend.''

"Oh?" I felt this unwanted rush of hope. "I thought she was so wonderful. So superior and all that.''

"Well, she is a nice kid," he said quickly. "But after seeing her for a while, I find her a little tedious—if you know what I mean.''

"No, I'm afraid I don't, because I certainly haven't found Ralph to be tedious at all. In fact, he's taking me to a big dance Saturday night which should be really exciting. I'm looking forward to it.''

"You are?" I don't know if I was imagining it,

but I thought I saw a fleeting look of jealousy cross Lenny's face. "Well, send Ralphy-boy my best, and tell him to watch out. I could appear at any time, when you least expect it!" He laughed that infuriating laugh, and the antagonism between us flared right up again.

Here we were, enemies, trying our best to hurt one another. Enemies when we were once so deeply in love. It was sad.

I took special care getting ready for the Saturday night dance on City Island. I wore a new dress, an early birthday present from my parents. My skin, fortunately, looked presentable once I had put on makeup, and I added some lipstick and eyeliner, both of which I used only on rare occasion. The effect was to make me look completely different.

"You look wonderful, Linda," my mother commented as I stood before her. "It does my heart good to see you going out with someone nice, instead of that boy!"

I frowned. The last thing I needed to hear was a reference to Lenny when I was trying hard not to think of him.

"It's just unfortunate you have to go all the way out to City Island by yourself on the bus."

"Ralph would have come to pick me up, but I told him not to bother," I explained. "It's such a long way for him to come, and it stays light late enough now so I'll feel safe taking the bus. Besides, I'm meeting Cesca and the two of us will be riding together. I'll be absolutely fine! Got to run, now. Bye!"

I left the house before my mother could come up with anything else to worry about. I rounded the corner, heading toward the bus stop, when I heard a voice say, "You look terrific!"

Lenny was standing in front of me. He was dressed as if he were going someplace special, but he was apparently in no hurry. He was leaning against the candy store window eating a double-scoop ice-cream cone.

"Th-thanks," was all I could say.

"So this is the night of the big dance." He grinned. "I see you bought a new dress for the occasion, too. How sweet!"

"My—my mother bought it for me. It's a birthday present," I felt I had to explain.

"I bet she was thrilled to have the occasion to—having you date someone else, I mean."

"Well, to tell you the truth, both my parents are happy I've finally gotten over you and moved on to someone better."

He laughed at this. "Oh, so you're trying to tell me that little nothing I saw you with is better than I am? Ha! And I suppose you can honestly say that he moves you the way I do, too?"

He put his hand on mine, sending currents of electricity through my body. I could feel his eyes boring into me and was afraid to look up to meet them. The power he had over me was too strong, too frightening. The only defense I had over him was to stay mad. So, I made myself think of the cruel words he had said to me when we broke up, about how the girls from Queens were so much better than I was.

I shook loose from his grasp. "What are you doing hanging around here, anyhow, Lenny? How come you're not out in Queens with your wonderful Janice right now?"

"Janice is babysitting tonight. She told me to come out there later, after the kids are asleep, to keep her company. I wanted to get out of the house, so I'm just hanging around, killing time."

"Oh, babysitting—how convenient!" My blood boiled at the thought of it. I knew perfectly well what the scene was when a boy kept a girl "company" while babysitting. With no adults around, the making out could progress in no time. It made me feel sick to think of Lenny making out with another girl, doing those things he had done with me.

Trying not to show my jealousy, I glanced at my watch. "Well, maybe you've got time to kill, but I don't. I don't want to keep Ralph waiting. Bye!" I turned from him and began walking down the street as quickly as I could on high heels.

"Oh, Linda!" he called after me.

I whirled around. "What?"

"When you're dancing with Ralphy-boy tonight, make sure you don't spend any time thinking of me!" He gave me an all-knowing grin.

"Don't worry, I won't!" I stalked away, absolutely steaming. I was angry at Lenny for trying to get to me and twice as angry at myself for allowing him to.

"Leave it to Lenny to spoil everything for me," I said to Cesca as we rode together on the bus. Mike and Ralph had arranged to meet us at the bus

181

stop and escort us to the dance. They had promised to take us back to Cesca's by taxi when the dance was over. I was going to spend the night at her house.

"He's not here. He can't spoil your good time if you don't let him," Cesca pointed out.

"I know. But I can't seem to stop letting him. It's as if he's taken up residence in a part of my mind and heart, and I can't get him out no matter what I do. I thought I was doing so well, and then talking to him brought it all back again."

"Then what you've got to do is keep away from him completely," said Cesca. "And I've got the perfect way. Remember I told you my father has a friend who knows about this great summer job?"

"Uh-huh."

"Well, I got it! I'm going to be a mother's helper for the children of the director of a summer camp for the blind. The camp's not too far from the city, and it's supposed to be a beautiful place. When I spoke to the director, Mr. Bard, he asked me if I had any friends who might be interested in working there. You've worked with blind people before, haven't you?"

"Yes. When I was in junior high, we did volunteer work at a school for blind kids. I became friendly with quite a few of them."

"See, I knew you'd be perfect," said Cesca. "This is a camp for blind adults, and they have an opening for a waitress. The pay isn't great, but you'll be in the country all summer and get to use the pool and lake and all. The kids who work there bunk together in a big house, and there are organized activities, like movies and hayrides, for us as well as for the campers. There are plenty of boys, both high school- and college-age, working as bus-boys or counselors. Mr. Bard told me that all the kids who work there have a great time. It'll be the perfect way for you to get Lenny out of your system once and for all. What do you say, Linda?"

Say? Cesca had thrown this information at me so fast I didn't know what to say. Going away on my own to work at a camp with other kids my age did sound like fun to me, especially if I could be with Cesca. It sure beat going back to Eden Gardens, which my parents were considering doing once again. I remembered that lonely summer last year, and I didn't want to repeat it. But part of me really still wanted to stay in the city and work on becom-ing Lenny's girlfriend again. I told Cesca I would think about it and let her know.

Our conversation made the long trip go by quickly, and we were soon at City Island. Ralph and Mike were waiting for us as planned. They had brought us flowers to put on our dresses, which I thought was really sweet. Lenny had never bought me flowers. Ralph was dressed up in a jacket and tie and looked adorable. He held my hand as we walked, the way I always wanted Lenny to. He danced with me, dance after dance, the way I always wished Lenny would.

But as we danced, Ralph hummed along to the music, and somehow I found this annoying. The cologne he was wearing was so strong it made me feel nauseous. And as I looked up at his profile, it seemed almost alien.

What was I doing here? Why was I dancing in Ralph's arms when I belonged with Lenny?

I do *not* belong with Lenny, I reminded myself. I'm here because he broke up with me and because I enjoy being with Ralph.

I knew I was kidding myself. I liked Ralph, but my feelings for him could never come close to what I felt for Lenny. Ralph was just not enough to do it for me—to break that powerful spell that drew me to Lenny no matter what. I needed to do something more decisive, something that would really change things and give me the opportunity to break away from Lenny once and for all. Maybe the job at the camp would be the very thing.

Late that night, after Mike and Ralph had taken us to Cesca's house in a taxi; after they had kissed us good night in the hallway of her building; after Cesca and I had discussed how cute they were, but I had admitted that Ralph didn't have what it took to make me forget about Lenny; I told her what I had decided. I would call Mr. Bard for an interview as soon as I came home from school on Monday.

It was what I needed to do.

Chapter

Sixteen

I set up an interview with Mr. Bard at the Holiday Camp for the Blind's downtown Manhattan office for that Thursday afternoon. I discussed the idea of the job with my parents, and they were all for it. They liked the idea that I would be out of the city, on my own, holding a responsible position, and helping people at the same time. And, of course, they were happy that I would be away from Lenny.

I felt very grown up and very nervous as I approached the office. The day was hot for early June, and I found myself sweating profusely. I made a mental note to keep my arms down at my sides so no one would notice that my armpits were absolutely soaked.

I sat in the office, waiting for Mr. Bard and trying to concentrate on the English textbook I had brought with me. Final exams were coming up soon. It was still important for me to do well on them, even though I was leaving Tech. It seemed like forever until the secretary announced, "Mr. Bard will see you now."

Mr. Bard's appearance was positively intimidating. He was huge—over six feet tall and perhaps three feet in circumference. I was grateful when he told me to sit down. Sitting, the difference in size between us wasn't nearly as overwhelming.

Mr. Bard carefully examined the résumé I had written that stated where I went to school, my work experience as a babysitter and as a CIT last summer, and my experience as a volunteer at the school for the blind.

Even with the air conditioner going, it was still hot in the office. Mr. Bard took out a handkerchief and wiped away the sweat that was beading on his brow; I was glad to see I wasn't the only one affected by the heat. "So," he began, "I see you've gone to some very fine schools, so I have to assume you're smart enough. And your work experience and the fact that you've had previous exposure to blind people is definitely in your favor. Tell me, why do you want to work with the blind?"

I sat watching a rivulet of sweat, which had escaped the handkerchief, make its way down Mr. Bard's temple. My armpits felt as if they were glued together. Why did Mr. Bard ask me a question like that? It was so hard to put into words reasons for things that just seemed to happen in life, like the opportunity for this job. I wanted to have a pleasant summer working in the country with kids my age, not to make a commitment to my life's work.

But then I thought of what it had been like when I had first volunteered at the blind school. I had actually been afraid of the blind kids—unsure of how to act around them, embarrassed to use expressions like, "I see." But then I had gotten to know them as people, and after a while it didn't even matter that they were blind. I had learned a lot from that experience, but I realized there was a lot more for me to learn.

"I want to work with the blind for two reasons," I answered finally. "I think I'm good with handicapped people and can do a service for them. But truthfully, I get something out of working with them as well."

"Oh? What's that?"

"Well, it's a funny thing I discovered while getting to know handicapped people. Some of them have it so hard, you would think they would be bitter and resentful. But they're not. Most of them are good-natured, kind, loving, and appreciative. They manage to be happy despite their handicaps, and I don't really understand why. But I do know that they have something I want for myself: the ability to take whatever difficulties life may bring; to learn and grow from my experiences; and to be a better, happier person, no matter what I have to overcome. That's what I want to get out of working with the blind."

Mr. Bard stared at me as if this were not the answer he had expected, and then his huge face broke into a smile. "Well, Linda, I think you'll work out very well on our waitress staff. Come into the front office, and I'll have my secretary give you the forms to fill out and explain more about how Holiday Camp operates. I'll be looking forward to seeing you there before the first session."

Mr. Bard held out his hand for me to shake. It was wet and clammy when I grasped it, but I didn't care. I had gotten my first official job on my own, and it felt great!

As good as I felt about getting the job, I was quite aware that I still had three more weeks in the city, and that meant three more weeks of dealing with feelings about Lenny which I still hadn't resolved. This was made quite evident to me when I ran into Chris Berland the next afternoon.

I had just come out of my building when I heard a car horn honking in the street. I looked and saw it was Chris, driving an old, red Chevrolet. He pulled in by a fire hydrant to talk.

"Chris! Whose car is that you're driving?" I asked.

"Mine!" He reached out and slapped his hand against the door with pride. "My parents paid the down payment as a graduation gift. Isn't she a beauty?"

"Sure is." I was impressed. So far, Chris was the only boy in our crowd to get his own car. You had to be eighteen to get a license in the city, and it was so expensive and difficult to maintain a car. "How are you going to pay for it?"

"I got a job, full-time, down on Wall Street. It pays really well to start."

"You're not going on to college?"

"I don't know. I might take some courses at night

in the fall, or I might take some time off to see how I can make it in the world of work. School's not my strong point, you know; not everyone's like you."

"I know." I couldn't help thinking of Lenny when he said this. "Well, good luck with your job, Chris, and your car!"

"Not so fast," he laughed. "I called you over for a reason. I want to tell you I'm having a party next Saturday night. It's in honor of graduation, and also because everyone should be in the city now that the kids are back from college and those going away for the summer haven't left yet. I want to get everyone from the crowd together, just like old times. What do you say?"

"I don't know, Chris. I'm not sure anymore that old times can ever be recaptured. Besides, what about drinking?"

"What about it?"

"Well, last time we had a party at your house, some of the boys brought beer. I didn't like the way that turned out. Remember how obnoxious Billy got, ripping Donna's coat and all?"

"So. That doesn't mean that'll happen again. Look, Linda, drinking is a fact of life in our society, whether you like it or not."

"But Chris, you don't understand. I've seen how damaging drinking can be. I know what it's like to get drunk and be sick. I've seen Lenny's uncle's whole life destroyed by alcohol. I made up my mind I don't want any part of it."

"Fine. And nobody's going to make you drink if you don't want to. But you can't expect other people to always see things the way you do. What are you going to do, cut yourself off from every social situation that involves alcohol?''

I thought about that and sighed defeatedly. ''No. I see what you mean, Chris. I'm going to come to your party and not worry about what other people are doing, as long as I'm okay.''

''Good. I guarantee you a good time. And ask Roz and Fran to come, too, will you? I want this to be as much like old times as possible.''

''Old times? Huh! Doesn't Chris realize it can never be like old times again?'' said Fran as she, Roz, and I met later that evening to go to the library to study together. It was something we had started to do recently, something to help keep our friendship going even though we attended three different schools.

''There have been too many changes. Nothing can ever be the same,'' said Roz.

''No, but that doesn't mean we can't still have good times together,'' I said. ''Look at the situation with our friendship, for example.''

''That's different,'' said Roz. ''We're all girls. There aren't the same problems as in a boy-girl relationship. I don't want Sheldon as a boyfriend anymore, but I still don't like the idea of seeing him with Jessie. I don't think I'm going to go.''

''That's ridiculous, Roz,'' I said. ''You haven't been going with Sheldon for months. Isn't it time you start rising above those kinds of feelings and going where you want to in this neighborhood without worrying about whether you'll run into him?''

''Linda's right,'' said Fran. ''I'm going to go to

the party whether Dan is there or not. In fact, I'd like to see him again, just to test my feelings."

"Well, truthfully, I don't know if my feelings about Lenny are really ready to be tested at this point," I admitted. "But I'm going to go to the party, anyhow. And it's for the very reason I just gave you, Roz. I want to be free enough to go anywhere I want without worrying about anyone else, not even Lenny!"

Despite my brave words, I was nervous as Roz, Fran, and I walked together to Chris's house on Saturday night. Although this party was supposed to be for neighborhood kids, Lenny could easily decide to bring Janice along if he wanted to. And while it was easy for me to tell Roz she shouldn't mind seeing Sheldon with Jessie, I wasn't sure if I could handle seeing Lenny with another girl.

Fortunately, Lenny was not there when we arrived at the party. Without his presence, I was able to relax and enjoy myself with some of the boys I hadn't seen for a while. Since I was going to be a senior next year, I was anxious to find out as much as I could about life at the various colleges. It wasn't going to be long before I would have to make a decision about which college to go to myself.

I danced with Louie, who told me he liked going to school in the city because he was able to save a lot of money by living at home. I danced with Geno, who told me how great the social life was away at school. Then I danced with Danny, who had no social life to speak of, but still loved being away from home.

Danny started questioning me about my relationship with Lenny. I told him about my dates with Ralph and how this time I thought it was really over with Lenny. "Well, it looks as if you're going to have a chance to prove it right now," he said to me.

I looked up and saw that Lenny had come into the room, and immediately, my heart started hammering. That made me really angry at myself. Why, oh why, after all my resolutions not to let him get to me, did he still affect me this way?

I tried not to look at him and to pretend he wasn't there, but it didn't work. As if they had a mind of their own, my eyes kept seeking him out. I noticed he had arrived with Joel Fudd, but there were no girls with them. I was glad to see that. I also noticed Lenny looked particularly cute tonight. I wasn't glad to see that. I didn't need anything to make me more susceptible to him than I already was.

Lenny got into the flow of the party right away. He loaded himself up with snacks and went from person to person, greeting everyone and making funny remarks. But me he ignored as if I weren't there.

This hurt. Even after all that had gone on between them, Roz and Sheldon were still able to talk to each other at this party. Danny and Fran were acting almost as if they still liked each other. Even Billy and Donna were managing to be civil. When things were good, Lenny and I had more going for us than any of the other couples did. Why did the hostility driving us apart have to be so awful that he couldn't even say hello to me?

The dance ended. "Come with me, Danny." I

grabbed his hand and led him to a part of the living room away from Lenny, who was reloading his plate with snacks. I stood close to Danny and began chatting away about how I was looking forward to my job this summer.

Fran came over and soon took over the conversation, gazing into Danny's eyes flirtatiously as if she were trying to rekindle what used to be. I couldn't believe Fran. I knew she wasn't interested in resuming a relationship with Danny, but she still needed the satisfaction of knowing he liked her best.

Well, I didn't care. Actually, I was grateful to Fran for monopolizing the conversation. I didn't need to know that Danny liked me best, and I didn't want to have to worry about making conversation, either. I was too busy trying to regain my composure, which I had lost the moment Lenny had walked into the room.

"Dance, Linda?" Lenny's voice behind me was so unexpected that I jumped when I heard it. I whirled around. He took my arm as if I had already accepted.

"Tell him no!" my mind tried to tell me. But my body didn't listen. My body just fell into his arms as if it still belonged there and allowed him to lead me across the floor.

To be in his arms again. I didn't think I could stand it. The brushing of our bodies as we swayed to the music, the touch of his hand clasping mine, the nearness of his face, that special chemistry I felt with no one else. It was all so right! We belonged together. Once I was with Lenny, I couldn't fool myself any longer. Every cell in my body cried out that I loved him, and only wanted him to love me back as he did before.

I couldn't tell from watching his profile what he was thinking. Was this just a casual dance to him, something to prove that he, too, could handle it, or was he feeling the way I did? As I wondered, he unclasped his hand from mine and placed it around my back so that both his arms were wrapped around me. Now we were dancing as we used to dance, holding each other tightly, his chin against my forehead, our bodies moving as one.

For one brief moment my heart soared, thinking this was his way of showing he still really cared. But then I realized he was perfectly capable of acting this way for the fun of it, to play with my mind.

This thought got me so angry I pushed away from him. "Hey, why did you do that?" He looked at me, an injured expression on his face.

When I saw his look, I realized he was sincere. "I—I just felt like—uh, I needed to get some air!" I tried to explain.

"It is stuffy in here—so many people." He gazed around the room. "Let's go take a walk and get some fresh air."

His smile seemed perfectly innocent, but I still was unsure as to how to react. "I don't know. I came with Roz and Fran, and I really have to go back with them."

"No problem. We'll come back before the party is over. I only want to talk to you, away from all these people."

I agreed to go with him. "I'll be back before too long," I said to Roz and Fran. I saw them shake their heads in disbelief as I left the party with Lenny.

Chris's house was just two blocks from the river, and Lenny led me in that direction. We sat on the wall that overlooked the Hudson and the George Washington Bridge. It was on that spot that we admitted we liked each other, almost two years ago. It was there that Lenny had told me he still cared about me last year before I had left for the country. This spot signified important milestones in our relationship. What was he going to tell me now?

"Where's Ralphy-boy tonight?" he started out by asking. "Didn't he object to your coming to this party?"

"Of course not. We're not going steady or anything. Why do you ask? Did lovely, ladylike Janice object to having you come?"

"No, she couldn't. I decided I didn't want to see her anymore."

I felt as if a million-pound weight had been lifted from my shoulders. "No? Why not? Didn't you enjoy babysitting with her last week?"

"Truthfully, no. It was boring. I mean it was okay when we were making out and all, but besides that we had nothing much to say to one another. A relationship has to be based on something more than sex to sustain it, you know."

"I know," I said quietly. I was sure our relationship had been based on more than sex. I remembered how happy I could be doing absolutely nothing with Lenny, as long as we were together. But I didn't remind him of this.

"Besides, it was such a hassle going out to Queens all the time. Didn't you find it a hassle going to City Island?"

"I guess. But it's worth it if it means having a good time with someone you care about."

"And you care about Ralph, is that what you're saying?"

I hesitated. I wanted Lenny to think that I felt more about Ralph than I really did, but I didn't want to have to lie to him. "Well, sure I care about him. I mean he's nice to me and fun to be with, and has a nice house, and kisses fine, but—"

"But he's not me, is he?" Lenny brazenly asked.

I swallowed hard. "No-oo. He's not you. And after all, we were going together a long time. But he doesn't hurt me the way you did either."

Lenny chose to ignore this point. "Is he taking you out for your birthday next week?"

"My birthday? I didn't even tell him it was my birthday. I arranged to see him after school on Wednesday, but we didn't discuss the weekend yet."

"Good. Because I want to take you out for your birthday."

"You do? Why?"

"To make up for the rotten way I treated you. I knew it was wrong for me to dump you the way I did, to say those lousy things about Janice being better than you, which obviously weren't true." He took a deep breath.

"It's hard for me to say this, Linda, but I want

you to try to understand the way I feel. When I broke up with you, I was going through an especially difficult period. I was feeling down on myself because I had to quit that job, which I had been counting on to prove I could be successful even though I had been kicked out of school. My failure at the job made my failure in school suddenly seem real to me. I finally had to face up to the fact my life could never be the same again. I wasn't a kid anymore, fooling around, putting things over on people, having a good time."

"I know. This stuff is serious."

"But I refused to admit that to myself for a long time. It was easier to put the blame on the other things in my life—my mother, my uncle. It's not that they weren't causing an insane situation, but I didn't seem to be able to do anything to change that. There was only one major area in my life where I did have the power to change things, so that's where I chose to focus all my unhappiness— on my relationship with you."

"Oh," was all I could say. "I didn't know that was what you were doing."

"Well, at first neither did I. I went to that party out in Queens, and the newness of the situation appealed to me. New girls, girls who liked me right away, who didn't know about my problems and the way I'd messed up my life—it was flattering, and it was exciting. It took me a while to realize that none of it was for real. Janice didn't like me, she liked what I was pretending to be. I never told her about being kicked out of high school or the problems I had at home. She knew I was smart and assumed

I'd be graduating and going on to college next year, the way I was supposed to. I let her believe it because I wanted to impress her—until I finally understood she wasn't even important enough to try to impress."

"No one is, Lenny," I said softly. "When it comes down to it, the only one you have to impress is yourself. You have to be able to feel good about what you do."

"I know, and I didn't," he admitted. "That's why I couldn't come back to you, even though I knew I had made a mistake breaking up with you. I had to do something to make me feel good about myself before I could even begin to approach you."

"Well, did you?" I was afraid to look at him. I focused instead on the dancing lights of the cars crossing the bridge.

He reached out and touched my face, turning it so he could gaze directly into my eyes. "Yes, I did—finally. I managed to complete this term of night school and pass all my subjects. I got that job I told you I interviewed for; I start a week from Monday. Then, three days ago, I helped my uncle pack up his things and get on a bus to Washington, hopefully never to return again. The last few days have been much more peaceful at my house, which has helped me to think more clearly. And the clearer I see things, the more I realize that none of what happened to me was your fault. You were always the one stabilizing force in my life. I must have been absolutely crazy to throw that away. I want to make it up to you, Linda. Will you give me the chance by going out with me on your birthday?"

I looked into his eyes. What I saw reflected there erased all the anger and resentment I had been harboring against Lenny since he had broken up with me. How could I do anything to "get even" with Lenny, when he had already been suffering so much pain? I didn't know how I would have acted had I been put in his circumstances. Maybe I would have acted better than he did, but also I might easily have acted worse. He had made some mistakes, but he was really trying to get his life together; I could see it. But what was most important was the way I felt when I was with him. I loved him so much I couldn't deny it. No one else made me feel the way Lenny did. I didn't know if anyone else ever could.

I nodded slowly. "Okay. I'll go out with you for my birthday. But I'm not making any other promises, Lenny. We'll have to see how it goes from there."

Chapter
Seventeen

You're going to let Lenny take you out for your birthday, Linda?'' Cesca gasped with disbelief when I told her the news Monday morning before our math final. ''That's absolutely insane! You know how he affects you. You go out with him and he'll have you convinced not to go to Holiday Camp for sure.''

''No he won't. I haven't even told him about Holiday Camp.''

''Well, make sure you don't.'' She shook her head. ''You're hopeless when it comes to Lenny. He can convince you of anything. And if you back out of the job now, it'll make me look bad. After all, I recommended you.''

''I know, and I won't,'' I promised.

But Cesca was right, of course. Each time I saw Lenny, my feelings for him intensified, and the barriers I had erected to protect myself from further hurt from him began to crumble. And because this was the last week of school and I only had to go in for exams, and because Lenny had the week off before starting his job, there was plenty of time for us to spend together.

This week was a period of transition for everyone, a sort of breathing time between the ending school year and the coming summer. Chris's party seemed to act as a catalyst, bringing everyone back together, because more and more people showed up at the park wall to hang out and get in touch with what was happening.

For that week, it really was almost like old times again. Although we had all undergone changes, we still shared a common background and a common bond. We were the teenagers of Washington Heights. That was something we would carry with us always, no matter what separate directions our lives might take.

The positive feelings I had for the crowd served to further intensify my feelings for Lenny. Each day I spent with him assured me that he really did care for me, that he was truly sorry for hurting me the way he did. But a part of me still held back from opening myself up completely to him. I still hadn't told him about Holiday Camp, and I still kept my date Wednesday afternoon with Ralph.

He met me at Tech after my last exam was over. He wanted me to go back to City Island with him, but I couldn't handle that. After having been so close to Lenny the past few days, the very idea of making out with Ralph turned me off.

"Why don't we do something outdoors?" I suggested. "How about the Bronx Zoo? Today's a perfect day for the zoo!"

Ralph looked disappointed, but he agreed to take me to the zoo to see the animals. I had always loved going to the zoo with Lenny, laughing together at the funny things the animals did. Ralph and I followed the same paths, saw the same exhibits, probably the same animals I had with Lenny. But it wasn't the same with Ralph.

Ralph laughed at the animals, but he didn't really seem interested in them. He hurried me through the exhibits, and it soon became obvious that his main goal was to find a secluded place where we could make out.

He finally located one, in a wooded area far from the main exhibits. He led me behind a tree and began kissing me and running his hands over my body.

Making out with Ralph had always been a basically pleasant experience, especially that time at his house. But that had been before I had started seeing Lenny again. Now, with the memory of Lenny's kisses fresh in my mind, kissing Ralph was something I just didn't want to do. Gently, I pushed him away.

"Ralph. This really isn't a good place for this. Someone's bound to come by."

"Who cares? We don't know them anyhow." He leaned up against me and resumed his advances.

Now I was really repulsed. "Come on, Ralph. I mean it—not here!" I pushed him more forcefully this time.

"Then where?" he demanded. "You wouldn't come to my house."

"So, what's the big deal? I thought we had a date to go out together, not to make out."

"Well, we did go out! I trekked all through this boring, noisy zoo, looking at dumb animals the entire afternoon. Now it's time for the payoff!" He tightened his grip on me.

I tried to struggle free from him, but he was insistent. I decided it might be easier to give him what he wanted than to put up a fight. I kissed him back even though, by this time, I found his kisses almost nauseating. The kissing seemed to make him happy, so I blocked my mind from what I was doing by concentrating on something more pleasant. I pretended I was being held by Lenny, and the kisses I was tasting were his.

I guess Ralph must have misinterpreted my acquiescence as approval, because he began to intensify his efforts. He stopped stroking me outside my clothing and began inching his hands up under my shirt.

This brought me back to reality, fast. The last thing I wanted was for Ralph to be groping me here in the park. "Cut that out, Ralph!" I slapped his hands and pulled away forcefully.

"Come on, Linda. Don't turn me away like this," he pleaded. "I won't be seeing you all summer. Give me something to remember you by."

What I felt like giving him was a good kick, but I really didn't want to be enemies with Ralph. Once I was out of his clutches, I kept moving away from him. "Sorry, Ralph, but it's time for me to start back home," I called back as I took off for the safety of the crowded section of the zoo. "My mother will kill me if I'm late for supper."

Ralph caught up to me, all apologetic for trying to make me do something I didn't want to do.

"Forget it, Ralph," I told him. "There's a long summer ahead of us. We'll see how we feel about everything in the fall."

He followed me to the bus stop, still trying to apologize. "When will I hear from you next, Linda?"

"I'll send you a postcard from camp," I said as my bus pulled up. I jumped aboard without even looking back. I sank into my seat with a sense of relief at finally getting away from him.

After my experience with Ralph, Lenny looked better to me than ever. Although, sexually, Lenny had been the aggressor in our relationship, he had never forced me to do anything I wasn't ready to do. Our love life had progressed gradually and naturally, over a long period of time, with both of us wanting every step we took. Just thinking about it made me want to be with him again.

I guess that's why, the next afternoon, when Lenny suggested I walk him home to get a cold drink, I went right along with the idea.

It was strange being at Lenny's house after so long. My last visit there had been the day his uncle had told me Lenny was thrown out of school, a day filled with turbulence, anger, and fear. But today, with his uncle's presence removed and his mother at work, Lenny's house seemed almost a peaceful place. Memories of other times we had been there together, just the two of us, took over, and all I wanted was for it to be that way again.

Lenny had a soda; he gave me one, too. As if in a familiar dream, I followed him to his room. Before I knew it I was in his arms, kissing him, touching him, loving him the way I did before.

All the hurt, anger, and pain and the relief, tenderness, and love that had been warring in my head since the time he broke up with me came pouring to the surface. For the first time, I was able to accept and express these feelings, in both a verbal and a physical way.

I felt so close to Lenny, and we shared so much that day that despite my promise to Cesca, I felt I could no longer hide the truth from him. I told him about my job at Holiday Camp.

I expected him to be upset, but not to the extent he was. He stared at me with a look of pain and disbelief. "You're actually telling me you're voluntarily going away for the whole summer again, after all we've been through together? How could you, Linda?"

"How could I? You seem to forget the fact that you had broken up with me when I made these arrangements! I had no reason to stay in the city. The opportunity for this job came up, and it sounded like something I'd like. I'm considering working with the handicapped when I get out of school, you know, so it's valuable experience to get a job working with them now. It could do great things for my career."

"Career? You're only turning sixteen, Linda.

You have plenty of time to get experience for a career. You could change your mind dozens of times about what you want to do in life. There's nothing so important about this lousy summer job. I know you didn't have me when you accepted it, but you've got me now. It's not too late to back out. Tell them something came up and you can't get away this summer. Tell them your mother's sick and needs your help, or you're sick, or you're allergic to blind people—anything! It doesn't matter what you tell them, as long as you're here with me. Rediscovering our love for each other has been so wonderful. Don't ruin it all by going away!''

He looked at me with so much love and longing that I felt my heart and my resolve melt. Cesca was right. I shouldn't have said anything to Lenny until right before I left for the country. Then it would have been too late for him to get me to change my mind.

I had less than a week now before I was scheduled to leave for Holiday Camp. If I backed out it would be difficult for them to replace me, but it could still be done. Part of me did want to go there, but the part of me that felt strongest now longed to stay in the city, where I could be with Lenny like this every day. I had missed him so much during the time we had been apart; I wanted nothing more than to make up for it by seeing him every moment I could.

I told Lenny I needed some time to think about it. I would let him know Saturday night when he took me out for my birthday.

*   *   *

206

I couldn't believe it when Lenny told me where he was taking me: to the restaurant on top of the World Trade Center. I knew it was expensive, but Lenny told me not to worry about that. He had won some money playing cards and had saved it for my birthday.

I was very excited while getting ready for our date that night. My parents were excited, too, but not in the same way I was.

"So, it happened again. You're back going out with that boy." My mother frowned as she saw me put on the dress she had so happily bought me when she knew I was going to wear it for a date with Ralph. "It's unbelievable how much you put up with from him. Don't you have any self-respect?"

"It has nothing to do with self-respect, Ma." I sighed and tried to concentrate on applying my makeup. "Lenny was going through a tough period and thought that his problems were caused by going with me. Once he began to straighten out the rest of his life, he realized this wasn't the case, and he wanted to go back with me again. He made a mistake and I forgave him. What's so terrible about that?"

"What's terrible is the hold that boy has on your life. He can manipulate you into doing anything he wants. Why, I can just see him going so far as to try to convince you to give up your job this summer. Wouldn't that be a tragic mistake!"

When she said that, I could see myself turn pale in the mirror. I quickly brushed blush on my cheeks, hoping she wouldn't notice. "Lenny can't convince me to do anything I really don't want to do," I said with more conviction than I felt. I still hadn't made a decision as to what to do about camp.

Our date couldn't have been more perfect. Lenny had managed to get us a table near the window, where we could look out over the entire city, way past Washington Heights and the George Washington Bridge. We could see the sun set, and then, as darkness took over the sky, watch the windows of the city light up like tiny jewels.

Impulsively, I took Lenny's hand and squeezed it. "This is the most wonderful dinner I ever had, Lenny. Thank you so much for taking me here."

He smiled. "Hey, don't thank me. It's what I wanted to do. I want this to be the start of nothing but wonderful days for us, Linda. Now that we're together again."

A brief shadow dimmed my happiness as I realized this was an inference to my decision whether or not to go away. Although this was the night I said I would give Lenny my answer, I still hadn't made up my mind. I had tossed over the pros and cons of taking and not taking the job, and I had leaned one way or the other countless times. The only decision I had made was not to make a decision until the last moment. The right answer, I hoped, would then come to me.

I put the country out of my mind again and tried to concentrate on the beautiful evening. As the sky darkened, a few high thunderclouds moved in, and

I could see flashes of lightning within them. Ordinarily, lightning frightened me, but now that I was level with the clouds, I felt perfectly safe. It was amazing to see familiar things from an entirely new perspective and to find how different that new perspective made me feel.

Lenny took me home in a taxi, and we rode up the West Side Highway, which ran along the Hudson River. It was so romantic to be sitting there with his arm around me, watching the river as we approached the bridge. "This will always be 'our bridge,' no matter what happens," Lenny whispered.

He kissed me then, there in the taxi, and I thought I would burst from the happiness and joy of it. There was nothing that made me feel better than being with Lenny when things were good with us. I loved him so much! How could I stand to be without him all summer long?

When we got to my building, we stood in our usual spot between the second and third floors. I clung to him, wanting to hold on to the moment, wishing this perfect night never had to end. How I wished I could go home with him and spend the night kissing him and loving him. How I wished I didn't have to make decisions that were so very hard to make!

"Well?" As if reading my mind, he pulled away from me and asked the question.

"Well, what?" I stalled for time.

"You told me that you'd let me know by tonight what you've decided. Whether you want to spend the summer with me.'' He kissed me lightly on the lips. ''Or without me.''

''Oh.'' I swallowed hard. All the arguments I had been tossing around over the past few days seemed to take shape in my mind, lining up in columns for and against going to Holiday Camp.

On the ''for'' side was the fact that I thought I would enjoy the work and gain valuable experience from it. I would be able to help people and help myself, too. Then there were all the people who were counting on me to take the job—Mr. Bard, Cesca, and my parents—people who would be upset if I backed out at the last moment.

On the ''against'' side was the fact that I would be leaving Lenny at a time when he was starting to build his life again and needed me. I would miss him terribly, and he would be hurt and feel I had abandoned him.

All these were thoughts I had had before, and I still hadn't been able to make up my mind. So now I tried to look at the situation from a different perspective. I tried to see myself in each possible scenario for the summer, and I tuned in to the feelings from each one.

First, I saw myself in the beautiful countryside, talking to a blind person as we walked together. The sun was shining on his face, which glowed with the peace of those who had found acceptance, and this peace somehow transferred to me.

Then I tried to visualize myself in the city, but, surprisingly, this was harder to do. Perhaps it was because I really didn't know what I would do with myself if I stayed in the city. Summer jobs were hard to come by here; probably I could expect only occasional babysitting work. So I saw myself without any particular direction, waiting on the park wall for Lenny to come home from work. As I waited I worried about him: How was his job going; had he had another fight with his mother; would he be in a good mood when he returned from work or would he be frustrated and take it out on me? As I worried, a terrible tension grabbed hold of my body, and I could feel my stomach clutch.

That's when the answer came, the answer my head had known all along but my heart had refused to accept. It was as if that little voice were there again, whispering to me what was right for me to do, and I had no choice but to tell it to Lenny.

"Well, Lenny." I took a deep breath. "I wish you wouldn't put it that way—as a decision whether to spend the summer with you or without you. Holiday Camp is only an hour from the city, and now that Chris and some of the other boys are getting cars, you can come up and visit. Plus, I get a weekend off every two weeks, and I'll be able to come into the city to see you. It won't be like last summer when we were apart so long without even knowing how we felt about each other. This summer we can still be together emotionally, even on the days we don't see one another."

"So, you're going to take the job." His voice was like ice.

"Yes." Then I told him all the reasons why. I

told him about the pros and cons I had listed in my head, and I told him how the answer had finally come to me.

"If I stay in the city, I won't be doing anything for myself, Lenny," I tried to explain. "I'll be spending my energy focusing on you and whether things are going well for you each day. That's not a healthy situation for either of us. If I go to the country, we'll both have the freedom to do what we have to do, to learn and grow from our experiences. In the long run, that's what's best for our relationship. I feel it inside. And I have to go with what I feel."

I stared into his eyes, waiting for his reaction. I wanted so much for him to understand what I was saying. I wasn't rejecting him by going to the country. I was only being true to myself, and that had to come first.

To my great relief, his expression softened. "Well, I guess I'd better tell Chris to get his engine in tune. I'm going to show up at Holiday Camp so often, they'll think I'm part of the staff!"

I laughed and threw my arms around him. "Oh, Lenny. I love you so much!"

"I love you, too, baby." He smiled at me. His eyes were warm and liquid, and I felt the power he always had over me.

He kissed me then, and the passion was so overwhelming that once again I wished we never had to separate at all. But even as I thought this, I knew I had made the right decision.

Somewhere inside of me was a part of me that knew the path I had to take. As long as I was true to that part of myself, the decisions I made would always work out for me.

If it was meant to be for me and Lenny, this one would work out, too.

To find out how things worked out
for Linda and Lenny, look for
DEDICATED TO THAT BOY I LOVE
coming in February 1990

About the Author

LINDA LEWIS was graduated from City College of New York and received her master's degree in special education. *All for the Love of That Boy* is her seventh novel. She has written five other Archway Paperbacks about Linda in the following sequence: *2 Young 2 Go 4 Boys, We Hate Everything but Boys, Is There Life After Boys?, We Love Only Older Boys,* and *My Heart Belongs to That Boy.* She has also written a book about Linda for younger readers, *Want to Trade Two Brothers for a Cat?,* which is available from Minstrel Books. Recently Ms. Lewis moved from New York to Lauderdale-by-the-Sea, Florida. She is married and has two children.